Critical Praise for A

TALES OF THE OUT &

D1334718

- Winner of a PEN/Beyond Margins ...
- A *New York Times* Editors' Choice
- An *Essence* Magazine Best Seller

"As this new collection of short fiction (most of it previously unpublished) makes clear, the writer formerly known as LeRoi Jones possesses an outtelligence of a high order. Baraka is such a provocateur, so skilled at prodding his perceived enemies (who are legion) in their tender underbellies, that it becomes easy to overlook that he is first and foremost a writer . . . He writes crisp, punchy sentences and has a fine ear for dialogue . . . In his prose as in his poetry, Baraka is at his best as a lyrical prophet of despair who transfigures his contentious racial and political views into a transcendent, 'outtelligent' clarity."

—NEW YORK TIMES BOOK REVIEW

"A marvelously vital and creative mind at work."

—LIBRARY JOURNAL

"Baraka remains a prodigiously skilled writer. *Tales of the Out & the Gone* is an apt reminder of Baraka's unique ability to touch on politics, race, and identity in a biting vernacular style."

—TIME OUT NEW YORK

"In his signature politically piercing and poetic staccato style, Baraka offers a perspective on social and political changes and a fresh view of the possibilities that language presents in exploring human passions . . . Fans and newcomers alike will appreciate Baraka's breadth of political perspective and passion for storytelling."

—BOOKLIST

"Baraka's ability to load his words with so much artillery results from his understanding of storytelling . . . Though the resolutions are often delivered like gut-shot punch lines, the circumstances behind the varied plots are complex, and are something too few people take the time to confront."

—SAN FRANCISCO CHRONICLE

"Baraka makes his prose jump with word coining—'outtelligent,' 'overstand'—and one-liners . . . The humor and off-the-wall jaunts tackle real issues of race, otherness, and power with pointed irony." —NEW YORK PRESS

"This literary elder's work, no matter what genre, has never failed to excite, never failed to elucidate and examine the human condition with scathing insight . . . The book's charm lies in its tautness. No words wasted here. *Tales* commands you to pay close attention, lest you miss a great joke or a heartbreaking truth." —BLACK ISSUES BOOK REVIEW

"Baraka unabashedly steps on toes, but does it in such a way that you close the book thanking him for it. He bends the English language to his liking without stopping to explain himself, which is refreshing from both ideological and technical perspectives." —IDAHO STATESMAN

"The short fiction here shows controversy is nothing new for the last poet laureate of New Jersey . . . Baraka certainly hasn't gone soft." —TIME OUT CHICAGO

"*Tales of the Out & the Gone* displays Baraka's increasing literary playfulness, intellectual exploration, and passion for intuitive abstract language. The book introduces new readers to Baraka's groundbreaking and ever-changing style." —EBONY

The *System* of *Dante's Hell*

A NOVEL BY
AMIRI BARAKA

AKASHICLASSICS: RENEGADE REPRINT SERIES
BROOKLYN

Published by Akashic Books
©1963, 1965 by LeRoi Jones/Amiri Baraka; ©2016 by Amina Baraka
Introduction ©2016 by Woodie King Jr.

Originally published in 1966 by Grove Press/Evergreen Black Cat. In addition, portions of this novel previously appeared in the following publications: the first seven Circles in *The Trembling Lamb;* "Hypocrites" and "Thieves" in *The Moderns;* "The Eighth Ditch" in *The Floating Bear,* © 1967 by Diane DiPrima and LeRoi Jones; "The Christian" and "The Rape" in *Soon One Morning;* "The Heretics" in *New American Story.*

ISBN: 978-1-61775-396-1
Library of Congress Control Number: 2015934039

Akashic Books
Brooklyn, New York, USA
Twitter: @AkashicBooks
Facebook: AkashicBooks
E-mail: info@akashicbooks.com
Website: www.akashicbooks.com

LeRoi Jones and the Emergence of Amiri Baraka
by Woodie King Jr.

The System of Dante's Hell is an experimental novel by the award-winning poet and playwright LeRoi Jones, written some eight years before he took the name Amiri Baraka. The author's autobiographical journey is so heavily influenced by Dante Alighieri's *Inferno* that it begs the question: did the poet/activist Jones see qualities in Dante that would lead him to become Baraka, for whom art and politics were inextricably connected?

When Jones first arrived in New York City, he was searching for an identity and for like-minded artists, poets, musicians, and writers. As it often does, his search took him back to where it all started. From his childhood in Newark, New Jersey, through his time spent at Howard University and later the US Air Force, to his self-imposed exile in Greenwich Village in the mid-1950s, *The System of Dante's Hell* captures the young poet/novelist "walking in memory."

The walk is both vague and exciting to witness, as it foreshadows the emergence of a poet, novelist, and activist who would become a major force in American literature. Rereading it now, it is easy to rediscover his literary influences in Beckett, Joyce, Pound, T.S. Eliot, and the existential philosophers Hegel and Kierkegaard; his stylistic and political ties to other writers of the time like Allen Ginsberg, Corso, Ferlinghetti, Frank O'Hara, Olson, Bob Kaufman, Diane di Prima, Larry Rivers, and Nat Hentoff; and his deeper connection to fellow Greenwich Village exiles like Calvin Hicks, A.B. Spellman, Bob Hamilton, Steve Cannon, Harold Cruse, Archie Shepp, Leroy Lucas, and Roland Snellings.

In his 1984 autobiography, Baraka explained how his voice emerged from *The System of Dante's Hell*:

> *I consciously wrote as deeply into my psyche as I could go. I didn't even want the words to "make sense." I had the theme in my mind . . . but the theme was just something against which I wanted to play endless variations. Each section had its own dynamic and pain. Going so deep into myself was like descending into Hell . . . I was tearing away from the "ready-mades" that imitating Creeley (or Olson) provided. I'd found that when you imitate peoples' form you take on their content as well. So I scrambled, and roamed, sometimes, blindly in my consciousness, to come up with something more essential, more rooted in my deepest experience . . . I wrote in the jagged staccato fragments until at the end of the piece I had come to, found, my own voice, or something beginning to approximate it.*

This results in a structure of free association, in which each section has headings instead of chapters. For example, the heading "Gluttony" tells us: "This place is not another. Cold white sidewalks. Time, as intimate. To myself, beautiful fingers . . ." In "SEVEN (The Destruction of America," note the free association of riffs, not unlike Ella Fitzgerald scatting. In the heading "CIRCLE 8," I have no idea what LeRoi means by "Ditch 5" but I do know he comes to a beautiful and lasting observation: "I am hidden from sight and guarded by demons."

The journey into hell had already been explored by Milton, Virgil, and Homer, but found a new readership with LeRoi Jones. This new version was as experimental as freeform jazz and abstract art; however, now it was from an African American perspective. Hell occupies space in LeRoi's head. Hell is where white people refuse to see him. He is Black. In defending his humanity to white people, he cannot ever focus on his own Black self.

Hell is in his head and is the inferno of LeRoi's frustration.

When LeRoi Jones wrote *The System of Dante's Hell*, America had not yet witnessed the Watts Riots, Malcolm had not been assassinated, the Black Arts Movement was not in ascendance, and LeRoi Jones had not yet become known as Amiri Baraka. Some fifty years later, we can see the spirit of these events anticipated in his poetic and politically charged coming of age in the bowels of hell.

Woodie King Jr. is a producer and director of Amiri Baraka's plays. Most recently, he produced and directed Baraka's final play, Most Dangerous Man in America (W.E.B. Du Bois). *He is author of* The Impact of Race *and editor of ten anthologies.*

THE SYSTEM OF DANTE'S HELL

	Neutrals			
	Circle 1.	Virtuous Heathen		
	Circle 2.	Lascivious		
Incontinent	Circle 3.	Gluttons		
	Circle 4.	Avaricious and Prodigal		
	Circle 5.	Wrathful		
	Circle 6.	Heretics*		
		(1) Violent against others		
Violent	Circle 7.	(2) Violent against self		
		(3) Violent against God, nature, and art		
			(1)	Panderers and Seducers
			(2)	Flatterers
			(3)	Simonists
			(4)	Diviners
	Circle 8.	Simply	(5)	Barrators
		Fraudulent	(6)	Hypocrites
			(7)	Thieves
			(8)	Fraudulent Counsellors
			(9)	Makers of discord
			(10)	Falsifiers
			(1)	to kindred
			(2)	to country and cause
	Circle 9.	Treacherous	(3)	to guests
			(4)	to lords and benefactors

"I put The Heretics in the deepest part of hell, though Dante had them spared, on higher ground.

It is heresy, against one's own sources, running in terror, from one's deepest responses and insights . . . the denial of feeling . . . that I see as basest evil.

We are not talking merely about *beliefs*, which are later, after the fact of feeling. A flower, turning from moisture and sun would turn evil colors and die.

NEUTRALS: The Vestibule

But Dante's hell is heaven. Look at things in another light.
Not always the smarting blue glare pressing through the
glass. Another light, or darkness. Wherever we'd go to rest.
By the simple rivers of our time. Dark cold water slapping
long wooden logs jammed 10 yards down in the weird slime,
6 or 12 of them hold up a pier. Water, wherever we'd rest.
And the first sun we see each other in. Long shadows down
off the top where we were. Down thru gray morning shrubs
and low cries of waked up animals.

Neutrals: The breakup
of my sensibility. First the doors. The brown night rolling
down bricks. Chipped stone stairs in the silence. Vegetables
rotting in the neighbors' minds. Dogs wetting on the buildings in absolute content. Seeing the pitied. The minds of
darkness. Not even sinister. Breaking out in tears along the
sidewalks of the season. Gray leaves outside the junkshop.
Sheridan Square blue men under thick quivering smoke.
Trees, statues in a background of voices. Justice, Égalité.
Horns break the fog with trucks full of dead chickens. Mo-
tors. Lotions.

The neutrals run jewelry shops & shit in si-

lence under magazines. Women disappear into Canada.
They painted & led interminable lives. They marched along
the sides of our cars in the cold brown weather. They wore
corduroy caps & listened to portables. The world was in
their eyes. They wore rings & had stories about them. They
walked halfway back from school with me. They were as tall
as anyone else you knew. Some sulked, across the street out
of sight, near the alley where the entrance to his home was.
A fat mother. A fat father with a mustache. Both houses, and
the irishman's near the playground. Balls went in our yards.
Strong hitters went in Angel's. They all lived near everything.

A house painter named Ellic, The Dog, "Flash." Eddie,
from across the street. Black shiny face, round hooked nose,
beads for hair. A thin light sister with droopy socks. Smiling. Athletic. Slowed by bow legs. Hustler. Could be made
angry. Snotty mouth. Hopeless.

The mind fastens past landscapes. Invisible agents. The secret trusts. My own elliptical. The trees' shadows broaden.
The sky draws together darkening. Shadows beneath my
fingers. Gloom grown under my flesh.

Or fasten across the lots, the gray garages, roofs suspended
over cherry trees. The playground fence. Bleakly with guns
in the still thin night. Shadows of companions drawn out
along the ground. Newark Street green wood, chipped,
newsstands. Dim stores in the winter. Thin brown owners
of buicks.

And this not the first. Not beginnings. Smells of

dreams. The pickles of the street's noise. Fire escapes of imagination. To fall off to death. Unavailable. Delayed into whispering under hurled leaves. Paper boxes roll down near the pool. From blue reflection, through the fence to the railroad. No trains. The walks there and back to where I was. Night queens in winter dusk. Drowning city of silence. Ishmael back, up through the thin winter smells. Conked hair, tweed coat, slightly bent at the coffee corner. Drugstore, hands turning the knob for constant variation. Music. For the different ideas of the world. We would turn slowly and look. Or continue eating near the juke box. Theories sketch each abstraction. Later in his old face ideas were ugly.

Or be wrong because of simple movement. Not emotion. From under all this. The weight of myself. Not even with you to think of. That settled. Without the slightest outside.

Stone on stone. Hard cobblestones, oil lamps, green house of the native. Natives down the street. All dead. All walking slowly toward their lives. Already, each Sunday forever. The man was a minister. His wife was light-skinned with freckles. Their church was tall brown brick and sophisticated. Bach was colored and lived in the church with Handel. Beckett was funeral director with brown folding chairs. On W. Market St. in winters the white stripe ran down the center of my thots on the tar street. The church sat just out of shadows and its sun slanted down on the barbershops.

Even inside the house, linoleums were cold. Divided in their vagueness.

Each man his woman. Their histories die in the world. My own. To our children we are always and forever old. Grass grew up thru sidewalks. Mr. & Mrs. Puryear passed over it. Their gentle old minds knew my name. And I point out forever their green grass. Brown unopened books. The smell of the world. Just inside the dark bedroom. The world. Inside the sealed eyes of obscure relatives. The whole world. A continuous throb in the next room.

He raced out thru sunlight past their arms and crossed the goal. Or nights with only the moon and their flat laughter he peed under metal stairs and ran through the cold night grinning. Each man his own place. Each flower in its place. Each voice hung about me in this late evening. Each face will come to me now. Or what it was running through their flesh, all the wild people stalking their own winters.

The street was always silent. Green white thick bricks up past where we could see. An open gate to the brown hard gravel no one liked. Another day grew up through this. Crowds down the street. Sound in red waves waves over the slow cold day. To dusk. To black night of rusty legs. "These little girls would run after dark past my house, sometimes chased by the neighbor hoods." A long hill stuck against the blue glass. From there the woman, the whore, the dancer, the lesbian, the middleclass coloured girl spread her legs. Or so my father said. The dog Paulette was on fire, and I slipped out through the open window to the roof. Then shinnied down to the ground. I hid out all night with some italians.

HEATHEN: No. 1

1

You've done everything you said you wdn't. Everything you said you despised. A fat mind, lying to itself. Unmoving like some lump in front of a window. Wife, child, house, city, clawing at your gentlest parts. Romance become just sad tinny lies. And your head full of them. What do you want anymore? Nothing. Not poetry or that purity of feeling you had. Even that asceticism you pulled in under your breast that drunks & schoolfriends thought of as "sense of humor" . . . gone, erased, some subtle rot disposed in its place. Turning toward everything in your life. Whatever clarity left, a green rot, a mud, a stifling at the base of the skull. No air gets in.

* * *

The room sat quiet in the evening under one white bulb. He sat with a glass empty at his right hand. A cigarette burning the ugly dining-room table. Unanswered letters, half-thumbed magazines, old books he had to reread to remember. An empty fight against the sogginess that had already crept in thru his eyes. A bare bulb on a cluttered room. A dirty floor full of food particles and roaches. Lower middleclass poverty. In ten years merely to lose one's footing on a social scale. Everything else, that seriousness, past, passed. Almost forgotten. The wild feeling of first seeing. Even a lost smell plagued the back of his mind. Coffee burning downtown when he paced the wet pavement trying to look intense. And that walked thru him like weather.

* * *

I feel sick and lost and have nothing to place my hands on. A piano with two wrong notes. Broken chinese chimes. An unfaithful wife. Or even one that was faithful a trudgen round me. Everything I despise some harsh testimonial of my life. The Buddhism to affront me. Ugly Karma. My thin bony hands. Eyes fading. Embarrassed at any seriousness in me. Left outside I lose it all. So quickly. My youth wasted on the bare period of my desires.

* * *

He lived on a small street with 8 trees. Two rooming houses at the end of the street full of Puerto Ricans. Rich white americans between him and them. Like a chronicle. He said to himself often, looking out the window, or simply lying in bed listening to the walls breathe. Or the child whimper under the foul air of cat leavings pushed up out of the yard by some wind. Nothing more to see under flesh but himself staring bewildered. At his hands, his voice, his simple be-numbing life. Not even tragic. Can you raise tears at an un-painted floor. The simple incompetence of his writing. The white wall smeared with grease from hundreds of heads. All friends. Under his hands like domestic lice. The street hangs in front of the window & does not even breathe. Trucks go to New Jersey. The phone rings and it will be somebody he does not even understand. A dope addict who has written short stories. A thin working girl who tells jokes to his wife. A fat jew with strange diseases. A rich woman with paint on her slip. Hundreds of innocent voices honed to a razor-sharp distress by their imprecise lukewarm minds. Not important, if they moved in his head nothing would happen, he thought once. And then he stopped/embarrassed, egoistic. A cold wind on his neck from a smeared half-open window. The cigarette burned the table. The bubbles in the beer popped. He stared at his lip & tried to bite dried skin.

Nothing to interest me but myself. Disappeared, even the thin moan of ideas that once slipped through the pan of my head. The night is colder than the day. Two seconds lost in that observation. The same amount of time to stroke Nijins-ki's cheek. One quick soft move of my fingers on his face. That two seconds then that same two if they would if there were some way, would burn my soul to black ash. Scorch my thick veins.

I am myself. Insert the word disgust. A verb. Get

rid of the "am." Break out. Kill it. Rip the thing to shreds. This thing, if you read it, will jam your face in my shit. Now say something intelligent!

2

I've loved about all the people I can. Frank, for oblique lust, his mind. The satin light floating on his words. His life tinted and full of afternoons. My own a weird dawn. Hedges & that thin morning water covering my skin. I had a hat on and wdn't sit down. Light was emptying the windows and someone else slept close to us, fouling the room with his breath. That cdn't move. It killed itself. And opens stupidly now like a time capsule. You don't rub your mouth on some-one's back to be accused. Move it or shut up!

(He was lovely and he sat surrounded by paintings watching his friends die. The farmers went crazy and voted. The FBI showed up to purchase condoms. Nothing interesting was done for Ne-groes so they became stuck up and smelly.)

All the women I could put on a page have the same names. There was a round bar where the bunch of us sat listening to the sea and a whore suck her fingers. That white woman who counted in Spanish.

My wife doesn't belong in this because she sits next to a ghost and talks to him as if he played football for her college. He wd know if he sat in a bare bright room talking his life away. If he sat, frozen to his lies, spitting his blood on the floor. If he had no life but one he had to give continuously to others. If he had to wait for Hussars to piss in his mouth before he had an orgasm. If he could fly, or not fly, definitely. If something in his simple life were really simple or at least understandable. If he were five inches taller and weighed more. If he could kill anybody he wanted or sleep with statues of saints. Nothing is simpler than that. If there were a heaven he understood or if he could talk to anyone without trying to find out how much they knew about him. His capes. His knives. His lies. His houses. His money. His yellow hats. His laughter. His immaculate harems for heroes.

Still. The black Job. Mind gone. Head lost. Fingers stretch beyond his flesh. Eyes. Their voices' black lust. The fog. Each to the other moves in itself. He loves nothing he knows yet love is on him like a sickness. Your hair. Your mouth. Your ideas (these others, these hundreds of others. Old men you made love to in foreign cities have been given uniforms and sit plotting your death in their sleep. All those people you've kissed. The lies you've told everyone. And you know there is a woman dying now because you will not murder her. Will not dive out of your darkness and smother her under your filth. She knows the old men.

The house is old and night smooths its fetters with screams. It rolls in the wind and the windows sit low above the river and anyone sitting at a table writing is visible even across to the other side. The shores are the same. A wet cigarette burns the brown table & the walls heave under their burden of silence.

HEATHEN: No. 2

1

The first sun is already lost. The house breathes slowly beside the river under a steel turn of bridge. Myself, again, looking out across at shapes formed in space. My face hangs out the window. Air scoops in my head. To form more objects, fashioned from my speech. Trees in the other state. More objects, room sags under light. My skin glistens like glass. Metal beads on the pavement. Eyes on mine. Slick young men with glass skin. Dogs.

He had survived the evilest time. A time alone, with all the ugliness set in front of his eyes. His own shallowness paraded like buglers across the dead indians. Some time, some space, to move.

All I want is to move. To be able to flex flat muscles. Tendons drag into place. My face, the girl said naked, is beautiful. Your face is beautiful, she had said, only this once in her dirty cotton dress. Bernice. Some lovely figure here in a space, a void. Completely unknown her stink. Dirty eyes slippery in dark halls. She lived under my grandmother and peed in the yard. Before the fire. And shouted in the movies under the threat of boredom and myself, who had not yet become beautiful.

Women are objects in space. This new sun, could define them, were they here, or sane, or given to logical things. The mind objects them. Sterile Diane. Not the red-haired thighs / and mad machine of come. Another beast in another wood. One who wore wings made of moths.

He sat and was sad at his sitting. The day grew around him like a beast. Large and vapid, with blue fur turned in the thick fall air. All those people were silent. Their voices grew thinner. Their heads shrank. Their shoes came untied. They had to tug up their stockings several times to make them stay. He was thinking about his enemies. The iron eyes they sucked in their sleep. His own image flayed & drowned mandala. Innocent breathing. These lost beasts hated his mouth. They would kill him for it.

George was a child in blue bonnet. He stood naked against a window and begged for Oscar Williams. The piano struck notes at random. The wind did it. Naked he was smaller than his blue bonnet. His breasts were red sores, hard & indelicate, tasteless as the wet hour bleeding. The sun had come out. The rain had stopped. It was not yet dark.

All the other times I know form crusts under my tongue and hurt my speech. I slur my own name, I cannot remember anyone's name who I thought beautiful.

Only indelicate furtive lust. Even intimacy dulled by some hacking silent blade. The knife of the lie. Lying to one's self. You are uglier than that. You are more beautiful. You have more sense than to kill yourself this way. You are invisible in my mouth & talk through my head like radios.

George would laugh & float 3 inches off the ground, in deference to the old man. Believing anything he told himself.

> You've done everything you
> despised. Flowers fall off trees, wind
> under low branches shoves them into
> quick chill of the river, the high
> leaves disappear over stone fences.

Frank in armor thrust out his sword. My flesh is stone but I scream and he cringes with grunts. He screamed when we were close and laughed at the night. Its wet insanity.

Diane disintegrated into black notes beneath my inelegant hands. She died. She died. She died. I walked out into the morning with her breathing on my face. I never came again.

More forms against the white sky. I remember each face, each finger, each dumb word against lips against my face. The words. The stink of insolence. Or even I backing away from the zone. The area of feeling. Where anyone can enter. Unawares, even the cautious sterile greeter.

Another man

walked through me like hours. Not even closeness of flesh. Not against this blue ugly air. Not against you or myself. Not against the others, their unclosing eyes. The fat breasted fashionable slut of letters. Her blonde companion in the sulking dugouts of stupidity. She clasped my face in her bones & kissed silence into my mouth.

THE INCONTINENT: Lasciviousness

Petrus Borel is the lascivious man. Doubt yourself before you doubt me. To lie to anyone: white birds low over the house, over the roof. Me inside under the same roof. Night for the birds. And the light here burns all night. Burning away the air. Animal life will die. The plants later, when all is stone or the insane reflection of sun on stone. White rocks for the world. From water to low beach houses, expensive paintings to please that young elder.

Leather jacket, glasses, lost outside of purgatory. (Passd the neutrals into the first circle. And then the blue air blows in. Biting his thoughts. The man at the bar with fat trousers & filtered cigarettes. In his brain, white etch. Mouths without pictures.

But to the next level: Minds, faces collapse on the pavements outside of bars like these. Next to the traffic. The white wax casualness. Make up under the canopy. "You wouldn't be able to see those birds at night." To know the numbers inside darkness.

Your mouth, like the street, a cavern. Siren. Full moon hung low over wood. At the green cold streets.

We were "downtown." Eclipse like metal, over the umbrellas, shrubs at high altitudes. And the doorman wd sit unconcerned in a white sport shirt.

Think to what you see. Even past, its origin in a dust we scrub ourselves of. A link. to white and yellow spaces.

The idea of space. Eyes rub at night under alcohol. The distance to the ceiling. Crowds of lives, I could picture a man saying, between us and the ceiling. The river would roar underground. Ministers would walk by the windows. People would write poems. No one would be kissing me or talking seriously about my death.

It was a picture of a street. Six slim trees. Without animal life beneath the airplanes. Planets of justice. The white beard of God. All is suddenly not commonplace. Now it is again. Sinks. Laughter. Brooms. Language. You are empty of me. You could not recognize sidewalks without me. Lucre of the blood. The image is cold, without space, a dead talking of earth.

Lascivious is to meat. They take it into their mouths. Meat. Blood on the paper . . . or in Fielding's head on the sidewalk. A thrust. The walls of words, intimate gestures. The street took his feet. The dirt sung in night's hook. The moon again, in the cold.

A rung of the law. To thighs, because blood seeps from them. Flesh/ to pure air. Black smelly hair. Coarse, or softer than touch. Each to himself, as the pure image. Nothing remains with me . . . except myself to each, as to himself. The pure image. Nothing remains. a hallway of night. In a heavy season.

Anger is nothing. To me fear is much more. As if trees bled. The hour hung in my flesh. Pure act. The lie under streets stomping mist. The innocence of myself. Of you, under me. Of each finger dying. Egyptians, Praxiteles, Lester Young. Sources, implements under the ugly sea. Bright lips to colors seeping through the warm day. It could die. And the lust in the world fashioned into snow.

Gluttony

(It wd be present or forward, or as
each thing turns toward us, the
brown heavy past.)

City is gluttony. Mind you! The sparks hiss and sun drips on leaves.

This place is not another. Cold white sidewalks. Time, as intimate. To myself, beautiful fingers. You stand so straight. The mob of buildings. Their factories. Our incontinence.

She cd die on the street with her stockings pulled up. Her letters, not to old men on the east side. Myself, the young. Myself, again, under the spattering leaves. The west is a bridge. We'll travel someplace wide open. Not that slow brown water. A river. Another blue eye washing our land. Water to the east. We leave under the heavy air. Still, and winter coming on.

Fog settles on the bricks in the junkyard. The old cars smoking. In summer, smoke raised over the cities, black in winters. The woman could die with her stockings pulled up. Black bulbous eyes. Filthy sandwiches, if you can remember. A boy named Thomas who drew well with perfect pencils.

Perfect, these paths. Even on cement. We march well

and head around the corner. A black catholic girl had written my name on a trash can. I love you I love you I love you. It was cold then, and I unwrapped my shiny badge. The birds' peace officer. Skinny legs against the red buildings. Telephones against the green braid rug. The warm radio. All their old voices.

That was a wide street where James Karolis lived. He died in a bathroom of old age & segregation. His nose was stopped up and he could pee all over anybody's floor. Mr. Van Ness wd stop by to shake my hand & soothe his bohemians.

You cd be the leader of this weather. If you ran faster & told those jokes again. 7 or eight boys slumped against the wall. Or under the jungle bars, the shadows wd get in your eyes. More faces. More leaves. A farm sits there for years.

What do you want now? The street disappears. Night breaks down. Dogs bark in blue mist.

The blossom, the flower, the magic. If my flesh is sweet, my mind is pure. I am awake in your cold world.

INCONTINENT: The Prodigal

On a porch that summer, in night, in my body's skin, drunk, sitting stiff-legged in a rocking chair. Vita Nuova. To begin. There. Where it all ends. Neon hotels, rotten black collars. To begin, aside from aesthetes, homosexuals, smart boys from Maryland.

        The light fades, the last earthly blue, to night. To night. Dead in a chair in Newark. Black under irrelevant low stars.

        On a hill night fades, behind the house. Silence. Unmessed earth. My feet, my eyes, my hands hung in the warm air. Foppish lovely lips. Allen wrote years later. A weeping wraith.

        Hung in words, lying saints. The martyrs lose completely light. That slow feel of night. Industrial negroes with cold rusty fingers.

        The steps of tears, or dust between tall shadowy buildings. Germans with bald heads. To go backward, or cross over, into what you mean. What becomes realer than mere turning of hours. Shadows on long afternoons. Silent mouths

Break out. The turn. Bleaker. In the cold, my lips and hands turn hard. Peacock. Lone walker of mornings. Box-cars of fairies tilted into night. Jeliff Ave. Where Beverly lived and her father grew heavy mustaches. On that porch, on that air, words. To disappear, and leave the maid sad in her mother's gown.

A summer of dead names. Early twilight hoots of birds beyond the buildings. Each excess past. Now, this other, to be a beginning. A walk thru sun on stone. The train stations bracking a few blocks from where I walked.

He wore glasses and sold greeting cards. The buses went up Raymond Blvd. and turned left at Academy St. The O.D.B. (Office of Dependency Benefits) of the burning dogs. The red house with clubs. The white woman fondling me in a sand pit. The boy with his hand in my pocket. My watch. The lies. Snot. Wind blows smoke across tar. Chalked names. We jumped off the garage and I put my hand between our old friend's legs. Today the leaves clatter & the sun weights my fingers.

The old houses were slums except mine. Even that high apartment the french girl died in. Wallpaper, and bebop orchestras at the first sex. "Do anything you want to me . . . but don't hurt me. . . ." Wool for the cold. The old man sold his gas heaters and I kissed Lenore in the hall. She went back to the projects and had some baby. Leaves blew through the empty playground. The bigboys beat the little boys. The sun itself was gray.

We skipped together . . . in school. Her brothers (this other one), were failures. But she pressed close to me and stood that way for hours. My fingers loosened and I wished I had curly hair.

More than this is some other doing. Some other word. The man turned away cranes toward his beginning. Olson broke, Allen losing his hair. The faces seep together.

Or feathers of sun. Their noise. Steam from the streets. A long shadow of my body, tilted across the street. Danny Wilson's. A union organizer lived across the lot, Pooky, an italian with twin sisters. Or an accordionist, or the tiny television showing leaves. Augie's effeminate hands, my womanly mind. Voice, under their shrieks. Murray and Ora, hard and living. In light, they still sprawl in light. A thin bar of shadow on the stone. They live in light. The prodigal lives in darkness.

I have lost those clear days. Blue hoops, more days turning at the rust. The short throw across field. The pit. Noses. Rauscher. Old Black Rag Picker.

And blind adventure, those fences, with the Germans & dotty faced Keneir. In summer that seems cold. A breath.

Did John Holmes really jump off the Warren St. bridge? But his legs healed and he watched us hump the big italian bitch in Sweeney's cloakroom.

Eliot, Pound, Cummings, Apollinaire were living across from Kresges. I was erudite and talked to light-skinned women.

Trains, parties, death in a chair. Come back or leave it. His heavy jaw fastened to yours, from unknown dustiness. Pure movement. Of which to place himself, as himself, in a wooden cell, looking down on blue fenced water and the statue of a colored man.

A black cloak of distance. A blue box of toys, or have it books and razors. Let blonde lips shatter on his face. Asleep under blue coats. Awake at night for any substance of lost day. Already past. Each second the blue air turns. Each invisible leaf. Each snowed down street. An impossible distance of shadows. Wool cloak of years. Not time, not ever time. Not to myself, a young fat-lipped corpse.

Tell your lies some other time. "Your parents still visit the child."

Wrathful

I had forgotten to run. But if you believed I'd cuss that girl out. Fuck you, he repeated in his chin. Behind his meat counter I think even later he admired me. The polack did, for what reasons my mother could tell you. We worked next to that hospital & worked for a fat old man that one summer in the garage with all those rotten potatoes. A long spinster. An ugly middleclass negro bitch laughing in the hot kitchen at my red wool shirt & new jeans. Because its "too hot." Liars. Gossips. Widows. Cooks. Lived in the basement & went around the corner to her inferior nephews.

A bucket of coal. She shouted that from her stairs. The Owl Club. My father's adultery. Bowling down Quitman Street. That old 3 finger man with the gas station. Andy. Is he still there? On Quitman St. Dolores, who sd to me behind her pimples. My brother is dumb, my mother is dumb, my father is drunk, but you're beautiful. Will you be a doctor & take me to the proctors. The movies. The ball games. & later we will watch television on our linoleum & throw apple cores out the window. A fat blind woman tipped me for bringing her cokes. I went home in the afternoon & fucked Beverly. She had a baby & hid its face in her lips. Her paintings. Her Vincent, not a white Frenchman but an old rag head from the south.

A belly rub, a christmas tree, a negro. Autumn, is correct always. In the dark instinct. They believed me, and told others. Their walks. Their love affairs. Their sun.

My substance dark & talked of now odd times when everybody's dressed up. Forgive me.

SEVEN (The Destruction Of America

                    The Dead,
are indians. White bones dust
in their jelly. Dead in the world, to
white dust bones.

                    And Riders,
                              coming toward us. The Gloom

lifting. Trees
blown back.
          Cold season,
                    of steel, colors,
                              cheap medicines.

I am, as you are, caught. Here,
is where we die.
          On this mountain,
                    Looking down.

We will die up here
in the cold.

White man white crushed stones. In the cold rattling. Small fires, from drills. These hopis, pimps, rattlers, strolling in blue sun. Were killed or tortured. Worked for the land. The sun, the wind Gods of our secret ocean. Break out. Now, the boat rattles against soft mud. Its destination printed in expensive inks, in the captain's pocket. That tall person squeezing among shadows. These streets echo. The flag, so late, still chiming on its pole. The cold draped above the buildings. No one there to watch you. Dirt shows thru the grass. Dead trees rot in penthouses. Dogs, mad at dust. The wind pounds white bones.

White man fedora smiles. Pink fingernails. Abstract death flowers. Color to live, he slunk. Away, the radio squalled & the weather got bad. She undressed and walked thru their ranks. A black feather like his teeth had clamps. Stuck out beyond his lips. My name, like Indians. Dead hard ground.
Violence

against others,

against one's self,

against

God, Nature and Art.

SEDUCERS

The cold light, even inside. Say Autumn. Say Railroad. Say leaves. Go back. After crossing the street. The tracks. Dark stones. Your own space, wherever. It was afternoon, when she died. Everyone lie. For Lillian. who never understood the seasons. My shadow against the marquees. The dark / and it clutched her. Lillian, so thin with my talk. Gifts against the cold. Her space, impossible to say. To define. That distance across the trees. Her park. Her friends.

The sun had slept on grass in the south. The sun had marked its time. Lillian. Say love. Say slept. Say place your fingers here.

There were, of course, parties. She came. I stayed in the metal halls, rifling the mailboxes. Grinning. Being popular. Dancing alone, or with those heavy fleshed men I forgot to tell most people abt. She would look out the window & identify us. Even in the shadows. Even from the roof, those myths, the beautiful naked speech.

Go away & try to come back. Try to return here. Or wherever is softest, most beautiful. Go away, panderer. Liar. But come back, to it. Those high wire fences. The brown naked bodies. They turned or hurt or walked or pronounced my name. Does the word "foots" mean anything to you? She would say. Before she got skinny and died. Before that colored girl wept for her. Her false screams among the buffets, the dingy saturdays of her lovers.

What is left. If you return? You deserve to find dead slums. Streets. Yellow houses near the tracks. Someone's mother still dying with an oil lamp. Hillside place.

They would know what to say. Even now. If they weren't afraid. Of myself. Of what I made myself. The blue and orange hills. Red buildings. He wd know, even in the hall, bent over money on the floor. Blues singer. Thin Jimmy with tugged up pegs. Headlight, does that word mean anything to you? Separate persons.

Kenny got old. My sister. The street. The garbage. Or the black walls & illiterate letters. To continue from that. Don't look. Don't go back there. You are myself's river. Blue speech. Kenny got old, I tell you. Don't go back. Look out the window. The television whines on their christmas. They thot I was rich. I thot the hall was dark. The light fixture shd have been fancier. I was not good to look at. smart tho. They thot I was smart, too. They expected something like this. These shadows.

Bubbles, does that mean anything. Artificial or not. Saturday or not. My birthday is Easter in church if I can get dressed up. Don't say it. That my suit will not be new this year. It'll be clean tho. It'll be gray covert cloth. It'll be pink & gray. It'll be short brimmed. It'll be a reservoir. A view of ourselves. Not as little boys. Men. Intelligences. Super Heterodyne Expensive radios. Zippers. Blue men like my father. Like those associations

The playground is old. Kenny is old. Headlight is old. I am not. I came back to see them. I am in a black room with my new shoes. The two women stare at me and the shoes. I am drunker than their world. They do not even hate me. They are amused. I am drunker than their seasons.

The Flatterers

.284, a good season. In the sun. In hell, my head
so much sun, and cold for this month. Cars too,
squealing at the clocks. Gone past. These hands,
the metal burning night / are pictures, dreams, cousins.

A good
season. Lost, the dust settling. On water, cobblestones,
porches. We sat there staring at the blue street. The restaurant. My lovers' drums. Heaps of night. "You are a young
man & soon will be off to college." They knew then, and
walked around me for it.

Tough fat poet hung in the custard
store. A marine. The silent brothers. Huge slick hands. They
all had. Except fat awkward William / eyes were flowers.
Bellbottom pants. Slate buildings.

"The woman that ran the
place was a grouch, & you had to stand up with the cold
wind blowing on your back. Her husband, I think, was a
postman . . . like my father . . . but darker & more from the
south."

Down low for the dirt. For the hands touch. The

backs of the hands, dug in the dirt. Straight at you. On tar, in those low fences. Murderers loose in the buildings. A severed head, bloody in the winter. Near anthony's house & those other guys . . . The Buccaneers. But later, summer, it bounced right & he swept it up, wheeling in the air to throw it toward first. They were tough.

Or, the air, again, cold sun, wheeling, with hands strained, sun full in the eyes, up & around, the ball leaving, toward the squat shade homes, they yelled. They yelled, at me. The ball rolling out. Amazed, they loved it. Even the weather. Our sweatshirts, and Ginger strolling on the tar toward the jews. (Who got locked in the bread box. With the cakes? The same place used to stink the windows up. Frozen bums peeing through the windows. For cupcakes. Jelly donuts. Adventure. We laughed about it.)

She looked at my legs. They had grease on them then, when I wasn't at the clock. The quick fingers & fear at cripple tommy, the hero of the projects. William cd beat me, for sure. In that big big gym I hid from my thighs. Too long. Strong gripping fingers.

What else. Lefty? You cd catch him in that park. More days strung out. Time & sun. He laughed about it himself, when those two bears waited outside the stadium. "Lenora sd that you were hers. Is that true?" Jo Anne. She got pregnant & somber. Like today, near father's hotel. Divine. The doctors lived near there & one of my dianes. Diana, really, & her tall dark mother & drunken aunts. That was like cellars. That smell, & big cars to boot.

Her father was white & died old with a big mustache. She wanted to make it with him, & was afraid I did too. She wouldn't fix the phonograph where my picture was. What did that photo look like? (I think I had a german bush then. Not as large as that time in Orange watching the fags dance. His hair was red & mine stylish. My mother sat close to me watching my sister die. She really did later, when I was away. She sent me letters begging me to help her. Help her.

Beverly was my size & that started it. In the slums. Even we called them that, but all my later friends lived there. Behind those metal fences, for the playground. I never went there much, or only at night, to dance, & walk that fat girl home. They were all hip & beautiful. Even now, coming to strange things. Like this mist pushing off the day, Strange. These strangers, are beautiful. Be wary of them.

The woman liked me. Smart kid, she told everybody. I was fucking Beverly a little bit. The head of my dick went in, but I learned later to put my legs between hers, & that made it easier. She smiled when she found out. In that wet cellar.

Spots. She never really was happy. Maybe / at the proctors with me because it was dark & she could laugh at stupid things. I killed her. She let me do anything because of it. Eat her years later when I learned. Too late then, she kept calling. Believed me dead or in "Porto Rico." I came back furious with her chimneys. Her father was right. After all.

Can you plunge into the woods?

Lying by the stoop. Sell those gas heaters. Cook that food. Clean that building. Go to church.

Do you really think you were sane always. What about that powder-blue suit. Or dry-fucking Dolores Dean in your grandmother's house. Dolores Dean, and her less fortunate baby, Morgan. Big belly. Calvin Lewis did it.

He cdn't really play, I bet. I know pinball cdn't. Garmoney loved me. He got fat & forgot who I was. Hauling boxes. Bowling.

Playmaker. Strange for him to say it. At Robert Treat? The Boys' Club. Some obscure move with the hands. Across from Diane. Blacker, less desirable earlier. Grew huge in my eyes after all that killing. (Murdered my mother, father, sister, all the grandparents & uncles. Stepped out of their bloody flesh, a sinister shadow waiting for hardons.) She thought she could handle it, but it drove her crazy. She got educated & learned to make artificial birds. Another father for me, then. Blacker, too, less desirable. He walked her, on his wedding day, to the roof, & made her take off her skirt. He told me later drugged & dying.

"Anything you want Miss Sweeney. Big-eyed Miss Sweeney." "She Got Some bigass eyes." Ora Matthews. William Knowles (after he climbed the gas-pipes & began drumming like Elks on the desk), Murray Jackson. The Geeks. Miss Mawer, also, but better. Crippled lady. What wd she say now. Suck my pussy, hero. Eat me up.

You left that. But the cold is back. The hard gravel. Dorothy Bowman. Donald Pegram. Don't limit the world. It grows. It bulges. It is bleeding with your names, your soft fingers.

Who do you think you are on that couch with the lights off? Her father? Her porch? Her long street behind the railroad tracks? You are a train. Her father's noise in his sleep, of the south, from his eyes, under the weather, for you. Separate, again. These radios.

In the dark, she was soft. In the cellar. In the bedrooms. On the couch. Even with my mother's voice. My mother. My aunt frightened of the girl because they were both ugly. My aunt Gottlieb. Oh what an ugly church that ugly girl goes to. My grandfather had died in a warehouse full of election machines. Does that mean it was Autumn? Or that I wore badges or made it with Aubry at Belmar. Aubry who?

They all turn out good. I did. The way this is going. Who? Go back. Turn. The door will swing open into sun. Into Autumn. Into the cold. Into loud arguments at night with the door open. Small children die. I kill everything . . . I can. This is This. I am left only with my small words . . . against the day. Against you. Against. My self.

The corner is old. Headlight, bubbles. Now. Look for the lies. Them now. They go away, these lovers. For my running. Those soft flies over the shortstop's head. Please. Not as a dead man. Even Diane. A fair second baseman. You let him die. No. The lies. No.

(Have they moved out of the city? I mean her tall beautiful mother & no good boyfriend)

                              Good field
                                       No Hit!

Simonists

Again, back. Dancing, again. The portions of the mountain under light and shade at noonday. Cf. *Purg.* iv. "When it is 3 P.M. in Italy, it is 6 P.M. at Jerusalem and 6 A.M. in Purgatory." Musicians crowd down the streets. Belmont Avenue, hung in front the hotdog store. The poet winds. Wine store, paint store. Buford & his brother. The National, more boldness.

Darkness. Shadows, the brown flags fold. Blue windows. Placards with large-lipped women. Lovers. You have a checkered swag, now cool it. Down the stairs. Pause on the stoop, to look both ways. The King of the Brewery tilted under night. A hill, for air, and my space. To Norfolk Street. The fag's boundary, they had a limit. Don't turn me over, please turn me over. Each his own area. of registration.

Beating them, in that bare light. He was humped over & his head bleeding. The lights bare, as his face. Bleeding. Simonist, thrown down from second story. They're dancing. The girl w/ wet clothes. A white girl in a rumba suit. A line of negroes waiting. To dance. Dis. The mirrors were blue, for her wedding, she slept on the roof. Jackie Bland & his band. Nat Phipps & his band. Magicians, falling from the heavens. Naked in the park. She had a blonde streak and weighed 5 stone. Lips. Hands. An alto saxophone. She walked into rooms. She knocked at yr door once you knew her. She drove a truck. Down the mountain.

Erselle sits there. Across, from you & the curled hair. He cd dance in that small room. A basement with sewing machines, and that was proper. His prognostication, in the shadows of the jungle gym was a leather jacket & lips swollen so bad he spit out yr name from the side of his mouth. Girls & hats. Those blue felts with gray bands. Bricks & garbage hands, across town. She stood there in the dark & waited for your fingers. My fingers. "Don't hurt me, please, just don't hurt me." Cross town. I cried, because we left. My overalls. My red shirt. My knickers. My picture like some wife years later in a coffee shop. Dressed in black. It was that easy because he was a musician. To say "She looked like a little mouse." That was me, tho. He didn't say anything, he just shut right up & told people I lied. I believed him, standing in front of the Italians, & felt sad at the season.

Dancer.

That was something too. Whistling. You want to be noticed. She asked you that question & made things come together. From whistling, things you danced to. Teddy & his golden boys. Spanish names. Their own women to line up, under that glaring light. The only light then. Dark, for them, now. They disappear. Under leaves? under words. Complete darkness, to penetrate. Your fingers are soft enough. But it's cold here & I keep my hands in my jacket.

Simoniacs, Simonists, Bolgia academic brown leaves.
3. The dancers. Mandrake, light suede shoes. Magic.

The Diviners

Gypsies lived here before me. Heads twisted backward, out to the yards, stalks. Their brown garages, stocking caps, green Bird suits. Basil suits. 15 feet to the yard, closer from the smashed toilet. Year of The Hurricane. Year of The Plague. Year of The Dead Animals.

Existent. This is Orlando Davis, who with his curly hair & large ass, steps thru mists everywhere. They caught him stealing on his scooter. They, the cops(?), moralists dropped on him from the skies. The music: Rachmaninoff's 3rd piano glinting. Remarkable thick weather he moved thru. Not as a woman this time, a sultry male. He looked tired, or bewildered. And they mobbed him at the river's edge, yelling their faces at heaven.

John Wieners is Michael Scott, made blind by God. Tears for everything. The fruit of his days in the past. Is past, as from a tower, he fell. Simon, dead also. Under various thumbs, our suns will pass.

This is past. Ourselves, under the earth. She made to get away. Thru Lorber's window, we passed ourselves. They were, in all, with me: Arlotta, Strob, Starling(?) and some-one else. At the same point, I leave to blaze in the elements. It was a labyrinth. Windows, broken glass in brown weeds. You kicked them as you walked, or rolled heavily if they threw you down.

Sitting across a river, they had fixed them-selves with tender faces. Years later I place my fingers on their running skulls.

If anyone ever lived in a closet, it was me. There were tracks, streets, a diner, the dark, all got be-tween me and their strings. "You're going crazy . . . in here with dark green glasses and the light off." It was a yellow bulb tho, and it all sat well on my shoulders. Vague wet air thrashed the stones. It sat well, without those faggots. Or ART, 5 steps up, in a wood house: a true arc.

That, and don't forget the canopied bed. The ugliest green draperies dragged and hooked across the bed. Action as completeness. If I hung out the window, it was warm and people watched.

A guy named powell who is a lawyer. Air pushing. Straight stone streets. A guy named pinckney who is a teacher. (Place again, those fingers, on my strings. Walk in here smiling. Sit yourself down. Rearrange your synods, your corrections, your trees.

Dolores Morgan, who had an illegitimate child**** PROSPEROUS

Calvin Lewis, who gave it to her**** PRIDE

Think about that: Michael at a beach, in the warm tide.

The figures I saw *were* fucking. "Huge" shadows, sprawling open their cunts.

Big Apple (myth says) knocked down a horse, split open a basketball player's skull.

For him, let us create a new world. Of Sex and cataclysm.

The rest, let them languish on their Sundays. Let them use shadows to sleep.

* * *

There was a pool hall I wondered about, an ugly snarled face, Jacqueline, money was no object for her probable Saturday walks. There were a few trees to circle, the pool hall, and slick Eddie. Also (because Eddie was only a later example) the first *Hipster*. Not Tom Perry in the chinese restaurant. Earlier(?) and in the sun. Saturday morning. It wd be cold & I was learning then to grow tired of the days. Special. I was layed out so flat, and lied, and loved anyone who'd cross my path. A few showed me unbelievable favor. A redhead maid with heavy lips. Worked for an exceptionally respectable faggot. Lived, with some ease, across from the beer barons, IT WAS HERE THAT THE GOLDEN BOYS FLED UP THE SREETS OF ROMANCE. HERE THAT THEY MADE THEIR HEROIC STAND AGAINST ME, ONLY TO SUCCUMB, LATER, TO MACHINATIONS DRAPED ACROSS THE WORLD. HERE, THEY THREW HANDS UP. AS IN CONQUEST, OR FINAL UGLY SUPPLICATION.

REVERE THE GOLDEN BOYS
& ALSO LOS CASSEDORES. THEY TRIED.

* * *

You can never be sure of the hour. Someone stands there blocking the light. Someone has his head split open. Someone walks down Waverly Ave. Someone finds himself used.

This is high tragedy. I will be deformed in hell.

Or say this about people. "They breathed & wore plaid pedal pushers." Can you say from that, "I told you so. Look at him, A bebopper."

"Lefty is pretty hip," he said to get me in. To the fag's house. Blonde streak. The Proctors, all interchangeable in the fish truck. Myth shd be broad & rest easily in branch brook lake. It shd rest like the black trestle between Baxter Terrace & The Cavaliers. (Some slight people thot that we, The Cavaliers, were the same as The Caballeros. Some other nuts thot that we were their (The Caballeros) juniors. We came long before them, but they were older and knew all about sex (so they influenced the crowd). We were still mostly masturbators.

Charlie Davis married Dolores Davis. (He cd do a lot of things tolerably well. Third base. 12 pt. basketball game before he got replaced. That was a blow. Beau Furr was much better, but he came from the slums & I knew him very obliquely (except that time he threw me all those passes & Big John said I'd grow up fast & tricky & "be a bitch.") And some of it was wasted on Peggy Ann Davis, i.e., that long weave down the sidelines (abt 45 yards)

PAYDIRT IS THIS:

Ray Simmons, shy & bony, will work in commercial art houses & revere me all his life. (Enough of his missed layups!)

Sess Peoples (it got thru to him, somehow, he sd "Stone-face," "Emperor," "You little dictatorial fart") as dark as he was & embarrassed by what he smelled on my clothes, Give the World. Let him march thru it in September giggling thru his fingers.

(Advanced philosophy wd be more registrations. Get more in. Deep Blue Sea. I, myself, am the debil.

A RANKING OF THE CAVALIERS IN THE ORDER OF THEIR PREPONDERANCE: (Ray & Sess done formal, as they are, floating in for the easy dunk.)

Leon Webster (came later, after the decay. My head gone, in new gray flannel suit (Black wool a nigger called it). Away, so far away, wings melted. Rome, if you want met-aphor. Use Rome, & Adams calls the turns. The Barbarians had come in. The cultivated & uncultivated alike. Sprawling thru the walls.) Suffice it to say he came from real slums & was as harsh as our enemies.

Morris Hines: As a compact, years ago under the shad-ows of those gray or brown buildings. Always heavier than his movement. Escape Bolgia in a buick. Left-handed first baseman: "Ingentes." Flatterer, even as whore Beatrice had her prediction, her Georges Sorel. We had our church. Sussex Ave. was rundown & all the negroes from the projects went there (the strivers after righteousness. American ideal, is not Cyrano's death on Lock Street. The poor went to Jemmy's church, but big Morris and his deacon father sat next to Joyce Smith's house every Sunday & their mother wd fan God. Malebolge (for the flatterers) for me, there is all you can imagine. Jehovah *me fecit.*

William Love: eyes are closed. (Was that Hudson St.? Warren?) He cd, after a fashion appear in Adams' class. He had short stubbed fingers he bit for his nerves. A butt. They called him (not our lovely names . . . these bastards like Ora, "Big Shot," called him "Bullet Head" or "Zakong.") I had fashioned something easier for his weakness but killers like Murray ground his face in the tar, & William wd chase him. Goof train. Rebound man, wheeld & for a time, as to the properties of his life, dealed. I'm told (and so fell into disrepute. In hell the sky is black, all see what the other sees. Outside the dark is motionless & dead leaves beat the air.

CIRCLE 8 (Ditch 5)   Grafters (Barrators)

I am hidden from sight and guarded by demons. And
    what?
You find me here, as a street. A tree, under blue heaven.

The time, elapsed, as fingers cross the cold glass. Your
    world
has sunk in space, immersed in romance, like whatever in
    my head

fastens dreams upon my speech. Nothing makes a silence,
    hands
slow or picking dutch thin blooms, wind shatters lips.

It was fashion. In and out of those yellow slate homes. Beds
there. Italians. "The monk," outside the movies. You had
forgotten about her streets. And frenchman's creek. Crit-
ters, are foreigners. You had forgotten all their blackness.
That tottering room you had only to open your mouth he
would have been in it, tottering. Like huge black figures cir-
cling the house. Lips, glasses & flags. Also like mad doctors,

skinny with acne. I slept several places, also with whores. But now now, this had done it. Years before things moved slowly. You had poets to get to. And then, some motions in the midwest. I traveled. From the Cavaliers, it was only then to schools. Downtown, I went on a bus, or uptown with a horn. Not the "gig" bag, but formal black peeling leather from the musky janitor's room. He was a southerner and called some guy "Sam." Jr. Collins had one, I thought, then. And someone looking like Dick Tracy (only, of course, the nose wasn't as pointed.).

But that was where the rodeos got in & Slick Andrew from the West. Dead Lillian called him Ungie, & he had a faggot brother who is probably sucking a cock right this moment. On Hillside Place or Waverly Ave. probably. Look him up, the next time you're in that city (or state).

This leaves out Becky, who rode buses and carried a buzzard's cup. This thing she waved, as my wife will, but then on that bus it drove me into my room, where later my uncle moved and my mother argued at his weight. I learned to jerk off, because probably there were no windows there. I think now there were, because I heard the Orioles sing "It's Too Soon To Know" through them, the window(s)), also, some outside girl, Woman, Willa Fleming. She was 26 then, and I 13(?) no, probably 14 and 15.

There was a dance up those flights over the polish man (now I'd say "polack"). Lenora was there and we got tight. Stuck up later, tho. It didn't matter then. Beverly met me near the playground.

A neighborhood house for underprivileged days. And we walked her home together. A whole crowd, including Frank the Liar. (A pitiful person. He too here, now, hid.

The Classical symphony. Second Ave., crossing the winter. Then, I walked, as if I grew old. Overcoats later, I still move that way. hands shoved deep in coat, in mind, what moves, as seldom the yard is green. Snow mounts invisible in the hours' air. Windows of slums chime with the cold.

This had past. This had come later. This moved, as sugar thru my fingers. As time, will. I prayed then, too. You can see it all from that street, like a grove of trees. Because it was quieter, even for them: we thot they were rich. And later, still her father had 2(3) jobs and all the clan moved in. Jews fled.

Ray moved in there later (that street) when it had run down, and the word had gotten out that Negroes were up the slopes. But Lennie was sweet too, and dark, and had a ruder humor. And Sess's brother Arnold too ugly and loud. Possessed of streets the moon missed.

You think you see? Famine there too. Driveways where the huge shadow of the King, his glass raised, rumbles under cars. All those houses went. Broome St. too. New myths? or fools die under the weight and cannot recognize their hands. New myth?

For Calvin, who has grown up thru the pavement. A homburg and huge cigar. Method Negro. Knives in our wealth, rape, that too thrown over. They scrambled toward the top. Summers mostly, to perform. I stayed at school and loved a girl named Peaches. (Not really, all ploy, and a Ford, and true love the Queen herself employs. If I were Raleigh, A negress would walk up my back.

        In Chicago I kept making the queer scene. Under the "El" with a preacher. And later, in the rotogravure, his slick (this other, larger, man, like my father) hair, murrays grease probably. He had a gray suit with gold and blue threads and he held my head under the quilt. The first guy (he spoke to me grinning and I said my name was Stephen Dedalus. And I read Proust and mathematics and loved Eliot for his tears. Towers, like Yeats (I didn't know him then, or only a little because of the Second Coming & Leda). But Africans lived there and czechs. One more guy and it was over. On the train, I wrote all this down. A journal now sitting in a tray on top the closet, where I placed it today. The journal says "Am I like that?" "Those trysts with R?" And move slow thru red leaves.

You could be distant then because of the weather. Space, now those thin jews live there and my brusque cuckold friend. Another bond. You miss everything. Even pain.

        Thin trees. There, it's so cold. Even downtown with pretty Negroes. Swimmers. Easter is past. So, I. The plan, to make it, On the Lam. You know. Me. These people never got thru. Once, in some rich spook's house, they played Rachmaninoff and I put it down. Not even recognizing what it was. The Isle of the Dead. Now, it can play and I can read, or pee, or think about my wife. It's gone, whatever smell rides in that air. Whatever time that was. However strong I was, who I thought I was.

A sideways time.

They fail tho. A woman now splits my face. Not what I am, who says that. Not what I am. My trips tho. Across town, or a few blocks away. Where I fell in final shame. At all of you. I don't recognize myself 10 seconds later. Who writes this will never read it.

IT IS FAILURE.

To love, if that were so. Look out the glass, at the yard changing. Trash blown across the fence. Disfigured voices.

You could be proper and know what to wear. You could look at shoes. You could find things beautiful on a radio. You could eat rice and be calm on a bus going to New York. You could write those white women and know the world had opened and birds died in your fingers. Or later, an italian almost saw me weep.

YOU LOVE THESE DEMONS AND WILL NOT LEAVE THEM.

Tho they are evil, food smells up the house, outside is cold, drugs addle the brain, hands cut and bleeding. Flesh to flesh, the cold halls echo death. And it will not come.

I am myself after all. The dead are what move me. The various dead.

Hypocrite(s)

Is/fear.
           At noise (beneath
the floor. Streets.
                    The very air.

You shout, or steal. The motion sure, the air, like sea pulled up. They'd cry in church so easy, so wooden & smelled up. Lemon oil, just behind the piano another room.

A door, just behind the last pew. The trustees filed in smiling. After they'd brought in the huge baskets of money. They'd smile & be important. Their grandsons would watch from the balcony (if you were middleclass baptists & had some women with pince-nez). Mrs. Peyton was one, but she stank & died skinny in a slum. They'd smile tho. Mr. Blanks. Mr. Russ. A dark man with a beautiful gray mustache. Also a weasely man (not the same one who'd announce things. Deacon Jones. The same as the song. The one who "threw the whisky in the well."

Bernice was a big usherette. Graves. They came in together and were beneath us. She smiled at me and wd have fucked at 13. Her mother watched me. Her mother was sly. Her mother was fat. Her mother liked that green statue of lincoln. Her mother gave me cookies and sd, "I married my first boyfriend." I wanted to know where the fuck he was. With lincoln, or working in the Adams' hat store. Easters they'd drag you in and make you buy pegs.

And black Betty. Stuck up, because she had "spanish" boyfriends (the golden boys, i.e., Teddy, Sonnyboy, Calvin, "and them") but the real reason I cdn't figure out. Her mother was burned and her sister stayed in the service. Shadows on those pavements. Boston Street, oil lamps, Orson Welles. A huge tailor.

They were all friends. Rufus the bootblack, low man on the totem pole. He had phone booths. Next to the florist. (The smart ones? I guess they thot that. Collier was the name. She was pretty at first but turned pale as wet wind. She disappeared one afternoon.

The old pimply-faced one went to some college and came back with bucks. His brother, younger, in the same high school as me and Jimmy. But he got out when it was plastic and Allen wore cardigans. He loved me because he knew I'd sucked his cousin off. (They were in league with the undertaker with the bad ear. Hayes. So, the hayeses, the colliers, Aubry, a woman with a child in the insurance projects. They were all connected. By blood, I guess. By ideas. By Jackie Robinson.

(There was also a spookier branch . . . included a pretty girl you'd see on shade calendars. The same ones they had in their florist shop. Roses and mixed daisies. Cheap flowers. Middleclass flowers.

Also, a mystery man who lived near the flower box. The refrigerator. I loitered there but he didn't respond. He knew about picnics and girls with rubber soles and good hair. He didn't tell me. He was Warren Slaten's style. Exposing me to softball in the suburbs and then showing up corny like that years later (in a nigger show) with a japanese pool cue and out of style clothes. A Square. And his mother worked in Klein's. Still, if you could say "South Munn Ave.," instead of Dey St. or Hillside Place or Belmont Ave., you had some note. You could watch ofays play tennis. You could come late to scout meetings and be made patrol leader of the flying eagles.

LeRoy was in it. Also Rudy. (Damn that he got in sideways, the Baxter Terrace mob. They had it going different. Not softball, not with the beautiful molded southern grass shiny money dear friend of sun walking smooth so far to talk quiet and knowing what it was to be something to live away and not know them. To not be me. To not know, finally, what it is that ran me. To come to this. To what you see here dying. To be that, and to be that, as I am, for you, for you all, for all space.

      But he was slum (Rudy) that was the difference. That I knew that . . . & we had erected by whatever guise . . . forget Morris . . . how he did escape is worth knowing tho: Barry got out, but that's understandable. His temperament was like mine when I go abstract and people talk nonsense to me.

BUT NOT EVER FOR ANY OF US AGAIN THE LOVELY WORLD OF WARREN SLATEN OR THE REALLY BEAUTIFUL PETTIGREWS.

And Rudy's mother was ugly and looked up to my grandmother, so that made him lower. Place. Place each thing, each dot of life. Each person, will be PLACED. DISPOSED OF.

Rudy and LeRoy were a team. Also "Red." That must have dragged them. To live in Baxter Terrace yet be made to join the "fags" troop because they went to the same church.

So they tried to take over as far as athletics, &c. Only Rudy was any good tho . . . and still not much compared to Baxter or my friends. So we controlled that easy. And I outside, still, without touching any of them. A long walk home, & they used my name as if I was old and my wife had gone out "walking."

It took place in a sunday school. The declensions. The age. Tomson, his whole top head caved in like Martin's publisher. And his stepson big mouth teddy (the bastard was shorter than I and weak as a bitch. Mark, his real son, was mongoloid.) liked my sister. He and later his friend (the music teacher) Freddy. A "closet queen." They both hunted easter eggs in the churchyard, and even planned to fuck fred's sister so I cdn't.

Get in close with me. If you're in mountains. Or weird smells pack your head. Cereals. Cold water.

"Gloom," Harvey called me. "Hi, Gloom." (If I knew what that meant. Or what became of him. His socks and shoes. His relatives. It wd be easy enough to predict the future. The past. The fireplaces and whores of the cemeteries of your linoleum.) This is tether. Push toward (SOME END.

It is static. It is constant. It is water. It is her lips. It is Aristotle's coughs in the tent all night in the snow. Why the old man lived to freeze us. His "reserve." Sandy, his name was. The same as the young wavy head jew I jabbed silly at camp. Also good body punches in the 2nd round brought down his guard. When he went down my first instinct was to run. But his brother congratulated me and thot he could kick my ass because he got a letter for band.

We did a lot of things, those years. Now, we do a lot of things. We drink water from streams. We walk down hoping to fuck mulattos when they bathe. We tell lies to keep from getting belted, and watch a faggot take a beating in the snow from our lie. Our fear.

Mutt the zipper. Mutt the zipper. Packed lunches, on Norfolk Street, beans, franks. The bus. Also a stone quarry. (That whole side I knew later, midnights, after work in a paint factory. You walk at night, fine. You show up. You sit. You alright. But you never be no doctor. (Hilary talking.)

Ora—Why you sit in the dark & fight me when I tickle?

Skippy—Boy, I'll beat your ass in Miss Powell's class,

cause Johnnyboy and I are friends and "Jones" did that dopey funny book about guys robbing everybody. I live in a cloakroom. I live where you tried to get rid of those Ledgers.

Knowles—Baroom, Baroom, Baroom-Baroom-Baroom. Sho, I'll stop or climb. Or smile, or hit, or fuck (maybe, I guess, because the inkspots were popular and he had that correct trill). Miss Golden gave you a "D" in dependability and she hated something in you.

Murray—Nothing to it. Just be around and need a clean nose and hit people on the back of the head. Don't look for me now. It's too sociological and'd make you cry. You playground step. "Brains."

Becky—(Ha, Ha, with colored teeth and tightass girlfriend. That was cross town. The masonic temple she gave me hunter and coke and it tasted like it does now.) Spread my legs on the 9 Clifton. Let you in for somethings. A new building to incest. Hymn to later masturbation. You could have had me, if you'd come down. Gone Down.

Love—Ah bullshit.

Morris—(*Later*) Boy, this cat is something. Is my dead sister. The car crashed her huge eyes. My father's big buick. You rich running. Pigeon toes, you got us in to the

Troops. (And those buildings, even tho Dolores, and
the two crazy ones, football players and midgets) were
crumbling. Were red, at the corner where my grandmother made "pageboys." Miss Still, was the lady she
worked for. The other street, where Willie lived, con-
tinued to the lot and the women's detention home you
could forget if you only looked at the tile store or the
abandoned icehouse full of ammonia. Jr. Bell fell thru
the floor. Jr. Bell died in the lake. Jr. Bell fucked Eunice before I did, or you. (In an alley behind the Zarros
house, also crumbling gray behind Central . . . You
pressed together.

Otis—We athletes. We bowlegged. We got crooked peckers.
We see'd you get stuck in the ass in a tent. We wanted
some and forgot later because you ran so fast and could
twist past the line for 12. I still know Whatley and he
still thinks you're a punk.

Gail—I'm fat, but Sammy likes it. Sammy and Wen Shi (&
Tomson). They dig. because their heads are sawed off.
I like Diane(a). Not her friends or spooky dead father.
She's old fashioned. You like her, LeRoi? Huh? Marcel-
line ain't (whisper) shit.

Marcelline—I don't even know what the hell you mean. I
had boyfriends and one even vomited in my mouth.
New Years, you never understood it. Did you jockstrop
bluejacket "foots"?

Sammy—I'm drafted and cool and wear an apron and we went to Coney last night.

Jackie Bland—You see me doing one thing (even tho you heard about me humping some chick in a condemned house) and you think you got something on me. Shit. I'm nigger stan kenton. I'm crazy. I got long arms and helped you whistle to juliet in the laundry (before they tore it down).

Nat P.—Intermission Riff. Is that what you know about Floyd Key and Allen Polite? You mean you never been to North Newark and met Scram and the cocksmen. Boy, we cool even tho we teach school now and disappeared in our powder-blue coats. (Billy can play better than you heard. You know Wayne? He played with us. You mean you never made the Los Ruedos? Wow. I ran track too, man, and waved my arms in sheer pinnacality.

JAN MANVILLE, MINNIE HAWKS, JUDSON, ALEX G.'S WIFE—Sylvia was part of our scene and you know she was hip. What about Holmes? He's a doctor now, and you know you admired him. He could run and liked to talk about sports. Caesar taught you to hurdle. He had great form. He's a doctor now too. All of us are somewhere. We own trees.

The Brantley Bros.—I'm a writer. I go to games. I knew you
when. I was impressed. I'm weird in Newark. I limp
like a tackle. I knew everybody. You wished a lot of
times you could have talked with my sister. You know
we don't understand what you mean by all this!

Yrs t.,
CAIAPHAS

Thieves

(Was I to have made this far journey, only to find the very thing which I had fled?—GAUGUIN/Noa Noa)

Space is cheap salves. A trombone in a penthouse. Madness over the phone. Dispute, if the thief live. If he be climbing thru our smashed windows his voice dragged in silk stockings on the radio; Greasy Head? The metal can clunks in the head, the radio says "duh, duh, duh-duh." Soft, tho. As pure impression—pure distinction.

The three pigs. The three Suns. Three Blind mice. Three of a Kind. To make ready. witches. B. for five. wives. letters. strikes. bases. women. The Magi, are popular. Are broken glass. vases, crisp, some soft faggot voice drowning the night.

It was a hall. Jazz, is that vulgar. Hooks, in the air, like sun. Tuesday's blue metal adolescence. Mutt the zipper, again, the fireplaces. Guns on Christmas. Strange vanishing toys. The brown house. Registers (old new? a closet behind the red chair.

* * *

The room was deformed. A heavy jowl, smell, softer hands than streets. The moon is bitter. crushing the banister.

A girl named Lorraine who used to go as our cousin— and then her tits came. She was a tall "zaaroom" face. Zebra. Mattie McClean. Her blouse back was loose. She had another name. Thin glasses, like some oyster ostrich humping. A gray house, next to Lorraine's red johns manville. Her mother and she looked the same except her mother was quieter, but they had the same hair. Lorraine smiled nasty. And smelled up the pool. Even lied about the nature of dances. And fumbled excitement near the park. (Lies or ignorance) birds like tar smile.

This jumble of houses' collars. Shined shoes. Show biz. BILLY— "O.K. vibe player, Blow!" ARNIE— Years later, the drain glows. Rhythms. Passports. We take our train to your astronomies. We evacuate sound. THE PAINTER— You Rat!

It could be run out. It could be yellow & black. It could have garages. It could be disinterested in its cement (or the years of cars that roll over my grandfather's grave.

PEGGY ANN— pigtails are for ugly girls. Snapshots, cotton dresses. To buy is to listen. To be had/caught/applauded in the smoke of our sound. In our Negro ulsters selling pot. In our language scared at the shadows of our crimes. DONALD— You're listening to the Symphony Sid Program.

But that, I told you musicians, the rooms we spoke of, that wind, Mere purity and light. This is sudden. Her red fingers. This is slant-

ing here. To me (houses tilt down into my memory. Cars.
Insides of mouths. I WANT YOU TO MEET MY FAMILY.
(rooms, aside, as this is. The door stands open. It did then
and my fat uncle strides in. He is 6 ft 4" and knew these
things in the spring of my thoughts.

Cardboard suitcases,
essays. Walked in broke and humble. On Cornelia St. "She
looks like a little mouse." Larry or I made that remark. The
windows were dull. Cold slush in their mouths. Nothing
got thru those clubs. The street would flow black, and a
moon.

Trees wherever you are is irrelevant. TALLEY— Muscles, some biographies. Nobody knows nuthin. You got nuthin on me, but my upbringing.

Which in effect, is where we come in. To prefer phone calls,
tassels on their shades (even from the street in Gramercy).
Bohemians around too. Certainly she is beautiful, to be a
lesbian, to be in stone, to be so close to my house.

Violence
to my body. To my mind. Closed in. To begin at the limit.
Work in to the core. Center. At which there is—nothing.
The surface of thought. Pure undulation at the midyear,
turned yellow as deserts, suns.

Cement room. stones, in
place. Fell there, perfect. For echoes, murders. Blood looked
strange on the street.

And there was that guy who wanted
to fight my father about the game. Spencer, his name was.

Tall & agile & dark. Skinny with long legs, low dangling hands on third base. I heard the language when I ran down to coach. Right near the fence, I could look across the street, and sometimes Danny would be out there, and I call him to the game. Usually the Davises (secret gypsies later making it as respectable shades). Algernon or Lonel(lionel), or pooky or fat (Jerome). Frank was the oldest, went away to Japan & got married. One girl, Evelyn, got fat and was transferred near the golf courses.

The woman, "Miss Davis" was the cruelest woman I know. Like Puerto Rican old women, the lower lip curls like dogs. Hatred or pure sight. Beast Fucci, wait like rachitic Algy for my baseball suit. Brown coarse gravel (if he thot my life was chrome. The orange house (Rev. Red's) large and not that first plunge into scum. Dead allies.

You defend them. But it is not the alley, or Elaine Charles. (She backed down, in some kind of pit. "It's too big." And I thought from that that white women had small holes. Racing car drivers. Pooky had the correct helmet, and Orlando would threaten him with it. He (Orlando) led the outriders. But merely elements of the street's imagination. I was center. He had strength and hair that would lay flat under tonics. And he rages with his snakes. His dirtiness. His pretenses at fucking. "Board" (Bud) was his other name. And I called him board and found out only later it was his mother's twisted lips. Even after they caught him with that loot.

THE SECRET SEVEN: (met under our porch and gave

parties—eating kits among the wet earth odors, rusted wet nails, footsteps.)

        EDDIE CLARK (cf. Vestibule) ALGERNON DAVIS (Board's brother) NORMAN SCOTT (cd run even with saddle head. Complete dust. Loosing, a slum in my own fingers. Earlier he made us laugh . . . "You mean those lidda mens?" Elks, we'd said. He was good w/ the little boys in Ringaleerio (as the whites say they sd different. Not our fays, they took their mark from us. Pooky wd say "rigaleerio" because his nose was stuffed. Dried snot on its edges. But Augie would say "ringy." Let's play ringy. He played w/ norfolk & Jay St. white factions as Keneir, Herbie Teufel, Johnny (who had strange staring fits the negroes were scared of), "White Norman" (to differentiate between him and Scotty) & sometimes the Zarros Bros. Charlie Johnny William and Frank. Frank was little for a long time but suddenly grew up big. Up thru the silent pavements. His brother I always had to watch. Augie idolized him. He was tough & fast & silent. Charlie Zarros was a scary name then.

        My sister Cassandra ELAINE. A confederate, lankier, bulging knees. Fast & that bitter decision to resist sweet life. Stale as death, her tears clog the hours.

The scar (a flab of cut skin like a halfmoon on her cheek. Like a photo a dead girl would clutch. Cry, those stale tears of time. An inch. A sudden light collapses around us. Illuminated we are "Dr. Caligari" or Orlando Davis. Beasts among reptiles. The huge flame of blasphemed God. Fucci screams from his lair, and we know, finally, his hurt name.

But she made good on all levels, except her lips were cold. And pouted—never like me, laughing wildly—or losing fights to J.D. in thick winter cold. (My father was ashamed that day. My hands were cold. "Frozen" Lois Jones screamed. Roy, his hands are frozen. Angel love him. Type. Move the blue file cabinets. She breaks down under pressure. Under this pressure (cool as blue steel in life and to the others, like Algy's—cruel. That power necessary—To Sustain Life. (Forever.

ORLANDO & ME. (Pre-conscious era. Bones of lost civilizations: the weird car I said I "built." Cd repair, from sheer radios. Listening to my lips chap. Wet patches on the paper factory. All the alleys back there. A maze. To disappear was what we wanted. To go out from here. Romantics. We wanted to split, the porch, even then. Beneath to caverns, slim romances.

The seventh person never came. Oh, of course, it was DANNY WILSON. (and his mother sad & cruel as italians. Hunted & hurt by perverted sons.)

LEROI, ELAINE, ORLANDO, NORMAN, EDDIE, ALGY & DANNY WILSON. (Fat afternoon saint. Eater of peanut butter & visitor at his sister's myriad "wettins."

THE EARLY PRE-DIASPORA CLAN (removed now from its beginnings. To the splints, slants, lies of later times. From that, e.g., KICK THE CAN. RED ROVER

(the theme "Red Rover, Red Rover, I dare you to come over")
usually at night, the moon low, a telephone pole just in front
of our steps. The Center. 19 Dey St. With a pole, right there,
for Hi-Go-Seek.

        HI-GO-SEEK. WAR. (i.e., not the cards, but
the street game where you mark the streets into countries.
MITCHELL 25921. (call me!) poor boy never had no phone
till then. About the time the money vanished off the buffet
& I sat weeping and peeing thru all the showings of THE
FIGHTING SULLIVANS.) That's how Algy got my suit, my
mother's wrath.

        I * DECLARE * WAR * ON * ETHIOPIA!
(cd be anybody. Peggy Davis even, when she played. They
took names of anywhere. Augie wd take Italy sometimes.
But everybody wanted to be America.)

MENU

14 packs of Kits
3 packages of Kool-Aid (grape or orange)
7 chocolate-covered graham crackers
7 Mary Janes

        (these were staples. And the parties were well
planned usually by Elaine, or Orlando who liked to eat. A
few outsiders got invited.

        Junior Bell— O.K., you got me! I'm
dead & a black myth. Poems should be written about me.
The myth of the cities Rise. (Black shadow against blue lake,
floats face down in the eternity of condoms.)

RISE. against
their dead bones. Restored to corridors, bus rides. The
simple dark.

   Eunice Reardon— Of course I know what happened. And I know that we weren't fucking (you & I) that
night in Charlie's yard. We had on all our clothes. You
pulled that stunt on your cousin. And used Jr.'s name as
some "symbol" of all evil. The black arts.

NEWARK ST. (snakes writhe in the ditch, binding our
      arms. Our minds are strong. Our minds)
 From one end to the other (Thos. Hardy begins, beneath
chains, shaking off sun, appearing a huge pier where our
brains are loaded.)
Its boundaries were Central Ave. To Sussex Ave. (1 block.)
This is center I mean. Where it all, came on. The rest is sub-
urb. The rest is outside this hole. Snakes die past this block.
Flames subside.

(Add Sussex Ave. To Orange St. . . . because of Jim Jam &
Ronnie & the cross-eyed girl who asked all new jersey to
"do nasty."

   (The slum LeRoy lived there also. 3 other Leroys.
Two Griffiths (who sd they were cousins. One, the tall dark
one, had a brother Robert who went from wet cowardice—

which never completely subsided—to hipster violence. THE GEEKS. As some liaison or at least someone who wdn't get done in. Like Murray. THE DUKES.

Where television and wine were invented. That strange wrecked house Carl (beautiful praxiteles) lived. Strange his life twisted. Charlie & he (& me too that warm summer we played & walked stiff legged). But they split up because he moved to a strange sad place. Made new friends. Treated us offhandedly. We never forgave him.

Carl Howard, his brothers, one of whom played brilliant ball. The short one with the bullet head. And for the great BURRY'S CO. team. He pitched. Carl played 3rd base for us. But he fell in with the Robt. Treat Crowd.

(Where they all teach now.)

In silence at the leaves. In deference to their mad forgotten lover.

* * *

JD STARLING, "STARING" JOHNNY, EUNICE & BILLY REARDON, JR. BELL, (old drunks 25, who still played on occasion & heroes to us, i.e., CHARLIE BOOZE & his brother, the slick head, Calvin. No, something else. A fabled pitcher, FRANK CUMMINGS (tucked his legs up but never made first string Central. Academic player for the playgrounds. I was faster & got more long gainers down the sides. "Comstu here" he said in "german" to impress us.

CHARLIE (and helen) PETERSEN. He was legendary black, but somehow made stupid awkward slow. Good natured but rusty. Disappeared when the new generation

(Slanty eyes who had it in for me & his sister Spotty Mae). Cambell their name was. Fast and southern.

THE ALDRIGES—Vivian (ubangi lips, later a tart, stupid whore. Rubber lips I called her also), Lawrence, the smart one. He probably works in the post office or collects debts for jews. Sammy (I hated. I wanted to blot out & kill when J.D. found out I was afraid of him (Sammy). Because the bigboys let me sit with them on the steps because I could insult anybody & win dozens constantly. "Your Mother's A Man." Separate, and sometimes abstruse. My symbols hung unblinked at. The surface appreciated, and I, sometimes, frustrated because the whole idea didn't get in . . . only the profanity.

And Lafayette, who set cats on fire.

That section of the street changed. Sociologists! Morons! Just past those cherry trees. Mary Ann Notare lived at the corner. & from there on Italians. Suddenly & without warning, they were all over. Those clean houses at the corner. How it slipped past me. What could they have said about me. Those old women sitting on the porch. The pizzeria on Sussex & Norfolk I never understood. (Until Morris moved there later.) The Armory was a block away from that bus stop. Years later I met Morris in his house after the summer cotillion. Respectable distance of years, educations. He had his finger cut off while I was in school. I saw him again crippled . . . wanting to know my new friend. Bumbling because he still wanted to play first base and by then we (the swag wearing middleclass spades of the town) were dancing. He

(& Leon & Snooky & Love & Earl) had come into it late. They were around the early belly-rubbing days & only earl, because he bought a cadillac, could begin to understand our stance. Our new heads.

Ellipse. These sudden autumns.

THE EIGHTH DITCH (IS DRAMA

(*Your tongues are fire
& your stratagems hell
itself.*)

NARRATOR—Tent among tents. Inner tent, dark/blaring sounds from outside. Too dark for shadows. Tho the moon is heavy, large, upon the outside of the outside tents. A wood floor. Beds strewn about, beneath the inner tent. Cries outside. Deaf ears sleep, heavy ruffling sounds. Men asleep inside. Four men asleep.

This is the first scene. Tho it is the end. Show it first, to give it light. As it shd be seen (BEFORE) as some justification. Some mortal suffering; slant the scene toward its hero's life. His black trusts. Together, we look in.

FIRST SCENE: *Same as above only afternoon. Two men sit on bunks. One is reading, the other stares at the book from across the room. The flaps of the tent are up, & we are looking in, at the two.*

46—(*Young, smooth-faced turning pages slowly. Absently*) Brittle youth, they say, I am dead america. And they know the season's change. I am as I am. Young, from sidewalks of wind. I think nothing of you, or myself, who has not yet come out. We wait. (*Looks up*) You & I, somewhere, to hear!

64—Call me Herman. (*Now at reader*) What do you feel. Grass? Games? False muscles cut thru water, thru precious sanity. Your earth is round & sits outside the world. You have millions of words to read. And you will read them. (*Loudly*) So buy expensive clothes and become middleclass that summer after college. But don't sneak away! You can't. I'll never know you, as some adventurer, but only as chattel. Sheep. A "turkey," in our vernacular.

46—(*Puzzled, looking up*) Things are joys even cut off from our lives. This was a field. A rough wood, they cut off. For loot mostly, impersonal. Buses of young sinister shadows herded into summer. So much of this will get lost. These pictures, of what sadness?

Who are you really?

64—The Street! Things around you. Even noises at night, or smells you are afraid of. I am a maelstrom of definitions. I can even fly. But as you must know, whatever, poorer than yrself. In hell, for it. If there is God. Or roofs where we lay under summer burning our minds. (64 *rises slowly, taking out cigarette, unbuttoning his shirt*)

46—You're not Grimsley. You don't shit under houses. I mean, you don't lie about who you are. I don't recognize you as anything. Just dust, as it must be thrown into the air. You'll disappear so fast. (*Sadly*) Can we talk about movies? What is it I shd talk about now? What shd I be thinking up? My uniform is pressed and ready. I sit, abstracted, suckling my thots. This is a siesta they told me.

64—(*Shirt open, crossing toward 46's bunk*) Forget your draperies. Your wallpaper. Television is not yet common. I love what is in me. These hours control our speech. You speak some other tongue. I understand your gestures. Your shadow on the pavement. Your strangeness.

46—What else can I give you? What else is as strong in me now. Bridges, smells. (*Pause, looking out the tent flap, smiling*) I delivered papers to some people like you. And got trapped in it; those streets. Their mouths stank of urine, black women with huge breasts lay naked in their beds. Filthy mounds of magazines, cakeboxes, children. I cd walk out of yr life as simply as I tossed newspapers down the sewer. It was Nassau St., mostly, and later the street where Skippy lived. Also Johnny Holmes. But that was cross town so I don't know if you know. I used to live in the insurance projects, right across from Tolchinskies pickle works. I almost killed myself twice around there. But we moved a couple of times since then. Even back here. Dey St. is where I live now & I control the Secret Seven.

64—Rarities. Elegance. Foppishness. Not really knowledge . . . tho I guess I wdn't know . . . actually. I take it as aggression . . . and hate you for it.

46—Do you think I'm rich?

64—It makes no difference. When you move to my neighborhood it'll be with a trumpet & school jacket. I have to make my move. I want to last, & this is the only way.

46—What do you mean? You want to last. How?

64—I want you to remember me . . . forever.

46—Remember you?? Why?

64—(*Smiles, now without shirt, and sitting on edge of cot*) I want you to remember me . . . so you can narrate the sorrow of my life. (*Laughs*) My inadequacies . . . and yr own. I want to sit inside yr head & scream obscenities into your speech. I want my life forever wrought up with yours!

46—You want immortality? Someone like you . . . You shd be happy you don't sleep forever in the vestibule. That you don't wipe your ass with newspapers or disappear into the marine corps. Damn. You know you cd turn up years later in a park studying *drama*. Thank whoever for that. You know it cd still happen!

64—I think not. Hah, even this much concentration has made my stock rise. Certainly these trees' shadows outside slant into my voice. That's enough to etch with certainty my fingers on yr lives. Your endless movings thru halls. (*Seriously*) But I want more. I will spread over you like heaven & push black clouds thru your eyes.

46—(*Turns on stomach reading the book again*) Perhaps, I *am* weak . . . but perhaps not.

64—(*Sitting on bunk begins to read book over 46's shoulder. As they are reading 64 places his hands on the other's shoulders, putting his face very close to the reader's*) What do you know? You sit right now on the surface of your life. I have, at least, all the black arts. The smell of deepest loneliness. (*Moves his fingers slowly on the other's shoulders*) I know things that will split your face & send you wild-eyed to your own meek thoughts!

46—Oh? I'm stronger than people think, I'm an athlete, and very quick witted. Ha, I'll bet you wdn't play the dozen with me. (*Looking up*)

64—No . . . I wdn't do that. You'd only make me mad and I'd have to kick yr ass. I want more than yr embarrassment! (*He sprawls his legs across the bunk, still holding the other's shoulders*) You still have to leave the country. You're not even out of high school yet. Paintings to see. Spend time in college. Spend money for abortions. Music to hear. Do you know about jazz yet?

46—Jazz? Hell yes. What's that got to do with anything?

64—You don't know yet, so why shd I bother. I don't know really. I never will quite understand.

But I do know you don't see anything at all clearly. Who's yr favorite jazz musician?

46—Jazz at the Philharmonic. Flip Phillips. Nat Cole.

64—Ha Ha . . . OK, sporty, you go on! Jazz at the Philharmonic, eh?

46—Yeh, that's right. I bet you like R & B & those quartets.

64—You goddam right . . . and I probably will all my life. But that's got nothing to do with anything. You'll know that when you narrate my life. I'll be a . . . . . foil! (*Slides down to where he is lying parallel to* 46, *hands still around his shoulders*)

46—Bellyrub parties too.

64—Yeh . . . I'm a bellyrub man! But that's my circle, now. I've reached my tether. I *am* static & reflect it meaningfully. But you, my man, are still in a wilderness. Ignorant & weak. You can be taken. It's 1947 and there are at least 13 years before anything falls right for you. If you live. (*Laughs*) I know names that control your life that you don't even know exist. Whole families of definitions. Memories. (*He moves his body onto the prone* 46)

NARRATOR—The mind is strange. Everything *must* make sense, must *mean* something some way. Whatever lie we fashion. Whatever sense we finally erect . . . no matter how far from what exists. Some link is made. Some blank gesture toward light.

     This is 1947 and all of you (*out the flap*) have not been born. Not yrselves I look at now. These ears, hands, lips of righteousness. This is a foetus drama. Yr hero is a foetus. Or if we are to remain academic . . . he is a man dying.

46—You talk like a man with a paper ass. (*Turns page*)

64—Hah, that's all in your head, baby. I talk like Morton Street, Newark, where I live now. Three blocks down from Hillside Ave. I talk like a hippy dip negro with turned up shoes. I talk like where we are. My friend, my honorable poet, you hear, exclusively, what you want. (*Lying on top* 46, *begins moving his hips from side to side*)

46—Are you Aubry?

64—No . . . I told you to call me Herman. Herman Saunders, from Morton St. An underprivileged negro youth now in the boyscouts. You're what's known as a middleclass Negro youth, also in the boyscouts. You knew all that. (*He loosens his belt and slips his trousers halfway down*)

46—Well that's senseless enough. (*Continues to read, but every now & again peering halfway over his shoulder at 64*)

64—Oh, don't worry. Don't worry. Hucklebuck Steamshovel blues. I Got. Deadeye, redeye, mean man, blues. I Got. Don't worry. Just sit tight. (*Laughs*) Or no, you better not!

46—You talk a lot!

64—Right, baby. Right, I do. I Got. Blues. Steamshovel blues. (*Begins loosening 46's belt, tugging gently at his trousers*) Blues. I Got. Abstract Expressionism blues. Existentialism blues. I Got. More blues, than you can shake your hiney at. (*Tugs harder at trousers*) Kierkegaard blues, boy are they here, a wringing and twisting. I even got newspaper blues. Or, fool, the blues blues. Not one thing escapes. All these blues are things you'll come into. I just got visions and words & shadows. I just got your life in my fingers. Everything you think sits here. Out thru that flap, the rest of your life. Hee hee, you don't know do you?

46—Oh shudup, shudup, willya, for christ's sakes keep your fat mouth quiet. (*Now tries to turn to get up from under 64*

*but the other has him secured and is pulling his pants down past
his buttocks)*

64—You name it, I've got it. Pure description, thass me. Pure
empathy for you, cocksucker.

46—What? What're you trying to do? I never sucked no
cock!

64—You did . . . but you wdn't want to know now. Ask your
grandmother. I mean about all those beaches and songs.
Singing for your supper. Hah. You don't have any of the
worries I got. I'm pure impression. Yeh. Got poetry
blues all thru my shoes. I Got. Yeah, the po-E-try blues.
And then there's little things like "The Modern Jazz
Blues." Bigot Blues. Yourself, my man . . . your stone
self. Talkin bout blues. There's a bunch. I mean, the 3
button suit blues. White buck blues (short short blues,
go thru me like wind, I mean, pure wind). I'm pure ex-
pression. White friend blues. Adultery blues (comeon
like you some dumb turkey, cool as you comeon to us,
like a stone turkey they had you in the new world). Got
what? Yeh, like love, baby, like love. I had the Kafka
blues . . . and give it up. So much I give up. Chicago,
Shreveport, puerto rico, lower east side, comeon like
new days. Sun everywhere in your eyes. Blues, come-on,
like yr beautiful self. (*Sinks down on boy, and 46 gives short
sharp moan, head raising up quickly, then, looking over at 64,
slumps head on elbows & closes eyes*)

Come on, man, wiggle a little. (*46 begins to move with the other, who is on top of him, pushing up and down as fast as he can*)

64—Oh, yeh, I came. I came in you. Yeh. (*Takes out penis and shows it to* 46) What's that make you think?

46—(*Still on stomach, looking blankly over his shoulder at* 64) I donno what it makes me think. Only thing is I guess I'll get pregnant.

64—(*Smiling*) Probably . . . so what?

46—How long will it take?

64—Not long, a few days.

46—(*Drops head on arms looking off outside tent*)

64—Now don't worry bout it too much. Take it slow.

(*Another youth comes into the clearing outside the tent. He goes to the tent and pushes the flaps back. Stands in doorway looking in*)

62—Otis. Oh yeh! (*46 tries to pull up pants.* 64 *backs away slightly*) Yeh. I know what you guys were doing and I want some. (*He unzips his pants and takes out a short black crooked penis.* 46 *pulls up his trousers and sits up on edge of bunk*)

46—What the hell you talking about?

62—You know what I'm talking about. Comeon (*Waves penis around*)

64—Look Otis, why don't you be cool, huh? Make it.

62—Whaddayoumean? Make it? You goddam pig, you want all the ass for yrself, huh?

46—Look Otis, forget it will you. Leave me alone, for christ's sake! Will you just leave me alone.

62—Leave you alone? Oh, yeh . . . now huh? After that goddam Herman bangs the shit out of you! Bullshit. I want some too.

64—Go fuck yrself, you crooked dick muthafucka. Nobody want nonea your crooked ass peter. Go jerk off.

62—You bastard. (*Goes for 46 but 64 grabs him and they wrestle. 46 runs thru the flap*)

NARRATOR—It comes back. What you saw . . . of your own life. The past / is passd. But you come back & see for yourself.

FIRST SCENE AGAIN: *Inside the tent. Night heavy in it. Four shapes covered on the bunks. Deep slow breath of sleep. A figure rises from a bed, and the moon throws his shadow twisted on the canvas. He moves across the floor, stopping at one of the bunks.*

64—(*Whispering*) Psst, hey. (*Shaking 46*) Wake up. Hey. (*Looks over his shoulder at the other sleepers. 46 turns slow in sleep and 64 climbs into his bed*)

46—(*Waking half-frightened*) What? Who is it?

64—(*Grins . . . voice made low soothing*) It's me, Saunders. (*He moves close to 46 and pushes himself onto the other's hips*)

46—What do you want? (*64 doesn't answer, just leans back away from the other, taking off his shorts then pulling down the other's pajama bottoms*)

64—Shh, don't make so much noise. (*He lies prone on 46. He begins slowly moving his hips*) OOh, ooh, shit. (*Makes noises thru his teeth*)

46—Is this all there is?

64—Yes. And why do you let me do it?

46—Because you say it's all there is . . . I guess.

(*Now the other two figures under the tent rise from their bunks*)

Wattley—Hey what's going on!

Cookie—(*Peering thru dark*) Yeh, hell, what's happenin captain?

64—(*Begins laughing . . . now making loud sounds for the others' bene-fit*) OOOOh yeh, get it, sweet cakes. Throw that ol nasty ass. OooO.

Wattley—Oh, man . . . some free ass. I gotta get me some.

Cookie—Yeh, hell, yeh. Hurry up, Herman. We gotta get some too. Uh-huh.

64—(*Still moaning and whining*) Ok, Ok, don't rush me. This is just gettin good.

46—(*Barely looks up at the others, turns his head looking out the tent*) What other blues do you have, Herman? How many others?

64—(*Screaming with laughter*) Oh, yes, yes, yes. I got all kinds, baby. Yes, indeed, as you will soon see. All kinds. Ooooh, thass elegant.

(WATTLEY *and* COOKIE *crowd around the bed harassing 64 and screaming with anticipation*)

64—Goddamit don't make so much noise!

(*Tent flap is pushed back and* OTIS–62 *comes running in*)

62—Yeh, uhhuh, I knew it. I knew you'd be gettin off some more. Well, goddam it I'm gonna get somea this.

(*He rushes toward the others. There is a melee*)

46—But what kinds, Herman. What kinds?

64—Oooh, baby, just keep throwin it up like that. Just keep throwin it up.

THE NINTH DITCH: MAKERS OF DISCORD

The Christians

Next to nothing. Next to the street, from a window, under all the noise from radios, 9 Cliftons, slickheads in bunches wanting to beat punks up, cops whistling, my uncle coming in the room, changing his collars, putting on checkered coat & 3 pens in breast pocket. I'd be there shining one shoe, taking out the bellbottom "hip" suit (some girl at the Y, a Duke chick, first called it that. And my friends ridiculed it not realizing that I was moved away. Spirit hovered over the big king, the polacks, and Springfield Ave. I knew already how to dance, & hit Beacon St. a couple of times, late, when it was nice, and rubbed sweaty against unknown Negroes.

My sister wd be somewhere in shadows pouting, looking down 4 stories at the chinese restaurant, & hump hatted cool daddies idling past in the cold. Snow already past our window quiet on the street. Friday, cool snow, for everyone cd run out new swag coats & slouch toward their breathing lives. And I'd be getting ready, folding my handkerchief, turning around toward the mirror, getting out the green tyrolean with the peacock band. Cool.

I knew I'd be alone, or someone cd be picking me up in a car. (Later, or earlier, we'd crowd in Earl's cadillac & he'd squirm thinking years later how to be an engineer, and confront me at my bohemian lady (who'd turned by now to elevator operator for a church. It shows what happens. I never got to fuck her either, just slick stammerings abt the world & Dylan Thomas & never got the Baudelaire book back either. But that's over & not yet come to. A horizon to look both ways, when you stand straddling it.

Belmont wd be jammed. And even in the winter sound trucks slashed thru the snow yowling blues. The world had opened and I stood in it smelling masturbation fingers. Slower, faster, than my time.

The hill slanted & blind men came up cold, coming out of the valentine store pushing snuff under their lips. Guitars blistering, the three kegs liquor store sides pushed out, and red whores dangled out the windows.

The bus came finally. 9 Clifton (Becky, her friend, sometimes Garmoney . . . and all the loud drooping-sock romeos from Central).

Friday, it was mine tho. White people fleeing the ward (from where?). Parties I didn't care about, old slick-haired cats from the south with thin mustaches.

The bus stopped & I looked out the window, or counted buicks, or wondered about the sky sitting so heavy on the Krueger (pronounced Kreeger) factory.

Down W. Kinney St., I knew I'd gotten out. Left all that. The Physical world. Under jews, for quarters, or whatever light got in. What talk I gave. My own ego, expanded like the street, ran under a bridge, to the river.

But after, loot against my leg, I'd move up the hill, thru Douglass, & finally up on the hill (unless I was late, taking meat out of Steve's window . . . then I'd pack into the Kinney).

It was contrast, doing things both ways . . . & then thinking about it all shoved in my head, grinning at my lips, & hunting echoes of my thot.

Central Ave., near my old neighborhood. (The Secret Seven, Nwk. St., The Boose Bros., Staring Johnny, Board, &c. yng pussies.)

From there, get out, rush across the street, the 24 or 44 wd come/wild flashes then with the frontier coming up. East Orange. Talk to anybody, but not now this was like Oregon. Or at least an airport now showing up loaded.

I barely drank tho, & it was the sharp air turned me on. Moving out, already. The project. But, again, alone.

No.

Nwk. was where the party was. Cookie's place. (They were hip mostly because they were foreign, for that matter, myself too. No one knew who I was in the ward. A hero maybe, with foreign friends. Pretty cool. Some kind of athlete. So when I came to places like that (in time) I'd show up loose, rangy, very nice. Somedays wind swept thru my eyes and I'd stare off whistling. This Was An ATTRIBUTE.

Al came down
from there to go to Barringer also Carl Hargraves, Jonesy,
most of Nat's band & a lot of freckle-faced negroes in Nwk.)

A balance could form then, could tear you up & set itself
so soon before you. The snow increased. Made drifts and
the wind was colder slammed snow against the streetlights.

The party was downstairs in a basement, impressive
for me because of Warren & my father's real middleclass
specters. Straight-haired lightskinned girls I met only at
picnics. There were some here, & some reputations got to
me peeling tenderness from my fingers.

Slanted lights, Ivory
Joe Hunter at Yvette's earlier. But her people naturally I
guess wd move in. Shadows were fascinating and I might
have danced w/ some anonymous american sweating when
I missed her feet. Stronger than I was. More sophisticated
in that world, that dungeon of ignorance. Snow veiled the
windows and the tin music squealed.

Barringer people, north
newark hoods (there were such, & I was, like the reputations, amazed. I loved the middleclass & they wd thrust
pikes at me thru my shadows. Everybody rubbed stomachs
& I stood around and wished everyone knew my name.

The Dukes were killing people then. They were talked about
like the State. Like flame against wood. They swooped in
Attila & his huns. They made everything & had brown
army jackets & humped hats like homburgs pulled down on
their ears. One knew Garmoney well, one got killed i heard

last month, one, a guy named rabbit who was lightweight golden gloves, loved my sister & turned up at my house for my father to scream at. We were rich I insist. (As Kenny or any of the hillside people cd tell you.)

No Cavaliers made these things, only, as I sd, occasionally Earl. All that had ended and I still didn't know. They envied me my interests and slunk outside the windows weeping.

So it was the end. Formal as a season.

Nine Chester Ave. Mahomet. The sick tribes of Aegina. Black skies of christendom, (the 44 pulled up near his house & I ran thru the snow right to the door. A blue light leaned up from the basement & high laughter & The Orioles). A world, we made then. Dead Columbus "its first victim." Spread out the world, split open our heads with what rattles in the cold. All sinners, placed against mute perfection.

They, the Dukes, came in like they did. Slow, with hands shoved deep in pockets. Laughing, respectable (like gunfighters of the west. When air stirred years later, and we rode out to the sea).

Now they spread out among us, & girls' eyes shifted from their men to the hulks sucking up the shadows. The Orioles were lovely anyway, & the snow increased whining against the glass.

SURE I WAS FRIGHT-
ENED BUT MAN THERE WAS NOT A GODDAMNED
THING TO DO. IN THIS CONCEPTION OF THE ENTIRE
WORLD OF TECHNOLOGY WE TRACE EVERYTHING
BACK TO MAN AND FINALLY DEMAND AN ETHICS SUIT-
ABLE TO THE WORLD OF TECHNOLOGY, IF, INDEED, WE
WISH TO CARRY THINGS THAT FAR.

They had taken up
the practice of wearing berets. Along with the army jackets (& bellbottom pants which was natural for people in
that strange twist of ourselves, that civil strife our bodies
screamed for . . . Now, too, you readers!).

So everyone, the
others, knew them right away. Girls wdn't dance with
them & that cd start it. Somebody trying to make a point
or something. Or if they were really salty they'd just claim
you stepped on their shoes. (Murray warned me once that
I'd better cool it or I was gonna get my hat blocked. I
was grateful, in a way, on W. Market Street: that orange
restaurant where they had quarter sets.)

Tonight someone
said something about the records. Whose property or the
music wasn't right or some idea came up to spread them-
selves. Like Jefferson wanting Louisiana, or Bertran deBorn
given dignity in Hell. There was a scuffle & the Dukes won.

(That big fat clown, slick, the husky sinister person,
bigeyed evil bastard . . . the one that didn't like me had a
weird name I can't think of and well-tailored "bells." Rabbit, Oscar (a camp follower) and some other cowboys.) They

pushed the guy's face in and the light, hung on a chain, swung crazy back and forth and the girls shot up the stairs. He, the n.nwk. cat, got out tho, up the stairs & split cursing in the snow. Things settled down & the new learning had come in. A New Order, & cookie clicked his tongue still cool under it, & I sat down talking to a girl I knew was too ugly to attract attention.

This wd be the second phase in our lives. Totalitarianism. Sheep performing in silence.

He came back with six guys and a meat cleaver. Rushed down the wooden stairs & made the whole place no man's land. Dukes took off the tams & tried to shove back in the darkness. Ladies pushed back on the walls. Orioles still grinding for the snow. "Where's that muthafucka." Lovely Dante at night under his flame taking heaven. A place, a system, where all is dealt with . . . as is proper. "I'm gonna kill that muthafucka." Waved the cleaver and I crept backward while his mob shuffled faces. "I'm gonna kill *some*body." Still I had my coat & edged away from the center (as I always came on. There. In your ditch, bleeding with you. Christians).

Now the blood turned & he licked his lips seeing their faces suffering. "Kill anybody," his axe slid thru the place throwing people on their stomachs, it grazed my face sending my green hat up against the record player. I wanted it back, but war broke out & I rushed around the bar. They tried to get up the stairs, the light girls & n.nwk. people. All the cool men bolted. I crouched with my mouth against the floor, till

Cookie came hurdling over the bar & crushed my back.

The Dukes fought the others. And were outnumbered (we wd suffer next week . . .) Nixon punched them (& got his later in Baxter with a baseball bat). And they finally disappeared up the stairs, all the fighters.

When we came out & went slow upstairs the fat guy was spread out in the snow & Nicks was slapping him in his face with the side of the cleaver. He bled under the light on the gray snow & his men had left him there to die.

Personators (alchemists) Falsifiers

If I am a good man, godfearing, brought from the field
to myself, in music, this round eye of mind, Jesus' flesh
is world to me, in words, thoughts heavier than myself.

If I were myself, at last, brought back

(the field turned
round
so it chatters under wind like leaves wave the day
back slowly.
Winter, for myself, the god man, the lover, who has
neither, nor

will it help sprawling, like this, across.

They had to shake my belief in the seasons. (If they could,
coming in here like that, drunk, cracks in the street, tar
taste. I could walk under those signs looking for their loves,
or run out, like later, and bleed to death of old age. I could
come back around those corners, down those hills (not saturday bright money, or the red-haired ladies of the consul.)
But bullets, and the aroma of Negroes, finally. All of them in
that movie, or living silently in pink houses.

* * *

So what becomes of me if Joe Louis and Roosevelt are caught here? As the leaves lay flat on the gray ground. As they will, each time I look. Wind in trash, moves. If they stand with me, as death will. As you can, lying flat and alone without me. As your love could, were it made of softer breath.

They are our life. As Gods, or the signal raised over the city. The bright planes, and smokes of the summer. The ball's descent, splendid, bouncing if I picked it up and made the proper move. So, smells sit around us, seducing our years.

* * *

Those 12 years of God, all strength followed (and the walks into halls, and their dusty windows. They would quote something, or remember who was who. Who was placed, made to enter the pure world of system. As our lives slip through the fingers of giants. Their voices ruling the radios. (Notes there dissolving. As prayers will. Now his mouth is shut. He will not pray again.

Fat, or how they moved. Sullen, lies about them later. To push it in. All, all, what he tasted in his bottoms. At his soul's hurt, days would crawl in place. Each thing at the top of buildings looking down, across to where he died. Years later this was.

But God should

be here. Should have his station, his final way of speech. More powerful than our dim halls, or the white mustache of the polack.

Hand could barely reach him. They'd scrape his chest / he pulled it back. Dancing away, left hand down. Shuffling. This God, on an orange porch, they listened with their sticks. Their travels out of hell, hells of the eastern city. Our country grew, its savages were given jobs. So it should, she wd laugh you to pieces, laugh you drunkenly at your hope.

He moved, and was with us in our shops. Our old men listened to the arms chop the air. Across the various yards, black gravel and white slat fences of the rich, who know nothing. Who are not jewish, even now they live where they do, with things around them grown to words. Their hands miss me. Their eyes twisted, packed with slender days.

The 12 years of God, are the last night. The Twelfth, that same thick evening air, summers, or when the last of the men got in. Winter, near christmas, they pulled in, swung down off their mounts. Shakespeare rattled drunkenly in the fog, folksingers, a thin Negro lying to his white girlfriend. Near parks, sitting cold in the scaly light like an empty room birds walk thru. Birds walk thru.

(And who was it drunk had told me unconvinced? His mother's rules. The groups walking with their trees. To make our proof . . . that there were Gods, whose world sat wet in the morning with our own.)

"So, I went for it. What the hell. Buncha drunks pissing on the corner. Plainclothes cat leaning out his black car window whistling. We move back toward the stoop. Turning both ways for Dukes." (Earlier or later, the cars would move away from the curb toward our lives. We had made it so far. This other group, my lieutenants, admirals, dentists.)

And they came thru it. Knew the punch, the stories, and how the doors sat open, and adults were ashamed to be so old they could not cry. They looked, if they would, or do now at what shows up saturdays needing a guide to place his life, his soul in their huge dark hands.

THE LATER GROUP

(if we die for the two big men. Satyr play shd move next! Change the scenery. Get the faggot off, and try to sober him up. Chrissakes. Clank (Airthefugginplaceout)

. . . WAS TP (Hollywood Ted & Co.) Everyone alive is a contemporary. As the man who beat Louis, or the Georgia heat where Roosevelt's head split. We know them together as part of our time.

And TP fit there. A Friend of The Family, really (as you people are now. Knowing so much). But I envied them, tony, sonnyboy, the rest. And it's so easy to cross them now. They've failed. Suppliants. Their dancing saved them those early times. Their coats. But it changed. The sun moved . . . our Gods, I said, had died. We weren't ready for anarchy . . . but it walked into us like morning.

So, look, for the first time at Anonymous Negroes and Harry S. Truman. (How's that grab you?) yall?) Anarchy, for a time.

Lucky, at first the war held. And we could think in that. I had a gun. But we didn't realize except what bled. And it had for youth. That when God is Killed, talking to oneself is a sign of nuttiness. (Our grandparents suffered.

And I watched them dance knowing that God was dead . . . and now, what it meant. I bought a checkered coat, green hat, kept alone, late, nights, till finally in a restaurant I met another man, and he stayed with me till my life was public.

* *

This lousy vaudeville group. (Historically, only a later development of The Golden Boys and Los Cassedores.) But the net had been drawn tighter. And new loves grew out of stone.

(A Story Of The New Group   **THE RAPE**

CIRCLE 9: Bolgia 1—Treachery To Kindred

I'd moved outside to sit. And sitting brought the others out. (The NEW group, I thot about them with that name then.) The New Group. What had been my distance. Looking across the crowd at the motion and smoke they raised. Jackie's listless band, exciting, in it. Junkies humped over their borrowed horns and sending beams of cock up niggers' clothes.

Now I'd move past. They had come too. To see me. Or see what the great "sharp" world cd do. Their white teeth and mulatto brains to face the ofay houses of history. THE BEAUTIFUL MIDDLECLASS HAD FORMED AND I WAS TO BE A GREAT FIGURE, A GIANT AMONG THEM. THEY FOLLOWED WITH THEIR EYES, OR LISTENED TO SOFT MOUTHS SPILL MY STORY OUT TO GIVE THEIR WIVES.

The fabric split. Silk patterns run in the rain. What thots the God had for us, I trampled, lost my way. Ran on what I was, to kill the arc, the lovely pattern of our lives.

Summers, during college, we all were celebrities. East Orange parties, people gave us lifts and sd our names to their friends. (What was left of the Golden Boys, Los Ruedos, splinter groups, and only me from the Cavaliers.) We'd made our move. They had on suits, and in my suit, names had run me down. Stymied me with pure voids of heat, moon, placing fingers on books.

Now, the party moved for us. And we made all kinds. This one was hippest for our time. East Orange, lightskinned girls, cars pulling in, smart clothes our fathers' masters wore. But this was the way. The movement. Our heads turned open for it. And light, pure warm light, flowed in.

I sat on a stoop. One of the white stoops of the rich (the Negro rich were lovely in their nonimportance in the world). Still, I sat and thot why they moved past me, the ladies, or why questions seemed to ride me down. The world itself, so easy to solve . . . and get rid of. Why did they want it? What pulled them in, that passed me by. I cd have wept each night of my life.

*   *

A muggy dust sat on us. And they made jokes and looked at me crooked, feasting on my eyes. Wondering why they liked me.

Sanchez, one of Leon's men, came out, whistled at the crowd of Lords, got his drink, and listened to a funny lie I told. He got in easy.

School came up, my own stupid trials they took as axioms for their lives. Any awkwardness, what they loved, and told their mothers of my intelligence. Still it sprung on them, from sitting in the trees. Silent with the silence; delighted in itself for thinking brutal concrete moves.

They Could Not Come To Me. It would be a thrust, or leave it home! Move the bastards out! A New Order(?) what came later returning to New York, to see Art, outside my head for the first time, and 200 year old symphonies I'd written only a few months earlier.

* *

A drunken girl, woman, slut, moved thru the trees. Weaving. I folded my arms and watched the trees, green almost under the porch lamp paste her in. They turned to me to see what noises I was making. Stupid things I'd thought I heard.

Foot slid down steps: up. Marking time, lime. Pulling at my tie, I watched and none of our girls was out. The party pushed noise into the dark. Only the cellar lights in the house spread out, light brown parents pushed their faces into pillows and hoped the party made their son popular.

She was skinny, dark and drunk. Nothing I'd want, without what pushed inside. They sd that to themselves, and to each other. What a desperate sick creature she was, and what she wanted here in their paradise.

And it took hold of me then. Who she was. Why I moved myself. Who she was, and what wd be the weight her face wd make. So I looked at them and crossed my eyes so they would think, for an instant, what I thought.

The chick was drunk. And probably some dumb whore slept to the end of the Kinney line. From the 3rd ward, she found herself with us. Trees. And the gray homes of the city, the other city, starting to fade on the hill.

She came to me. Direct. Even slit eyes gave me away. She moved straight. And paused to pat her coat. (Sanchez gave her a Lucky Strike.) She asked me with the fire making a shadow on her forehead where was Jones St.

We all knew that was Newark. And I had got the thing stirring.

* *

But how long till the logic of our lives runs us down? Destroys the face the wind sees. The long beautiful fingers numbed in slow summer waves of darkness?

Never. Never. The waves run in. Blue. (Our citizens are languid as music. And their hearts are slow motion lives. Dead histories I drag thru the streets of another time. Never.

* *

Five, with me. And the woman. Huge red lips, like they were turned inside out. Heavy breath, almost with veins. Her life bleeding slow in the soft summer. And not passion pushed her to me. Not any I could sit with magazines in the white toilet wishing love was some gruesome sunday thing still alive and fishy in my clothes. Still, smelling, that single tone, registered in our heads, as dirt paths where we lay the other ladies naked, and naked bulbs shown squarely on their different flesh.

I said, "Jones St." and that held over the street like drums of insects. Like some new morning with weird weather swam into our faces. The meanings, we gave. I gave. (Because it sat alone with me . . . and I raised it. Made it some purely bodily suck. The way my voice would not go down. A tone, to set some fire in dry wood. An inferno. Where flame is words, or lives, or the simple elegance of death.)

Sanchez showed his teeth (I think, he stood sideways looking at the car. Jingling the keys at the tone of my words.) The others moved. "We'll take you there." I almost fell, so moved that what I could drag into the world would stay. That others could see its shape and make it something in their brittle lives. "I'll take you there."

* *

Calvin, Donald, Sanchez, Leon, Joe & Me.
The Woman.

* *

They made to laugh. They made to get into the car. They made not to be responsible. All with me. (Tho this is new, I tell you now because, somehow, it all is right, whatever. For what sin you find me here. It's mine. My own irreconcilable life. My blood. My footsteps toward the black car smeared softly in the slow shadows of leaves.) The houses shone like naked bulbs. Thin laughter from the party trailed us up the street.

Sanchez threw the car in the wrong gear, nervous. It made that noise, and Donald (the dumb but handsome almost athlete jumped 10 feet . . . the others laughed and I chewed skin quickly off my thumb . . .) the woman talked directions at the floor.

Donald was at the woman's left, I at her right. The others packed in the front. Looking at us, across the seat. (Sanchez thru the mirror.) The whole night tightened, and it seemed our car rumbled on a cliff knocking huge rocks down a thousand feet. The thunderous tires roared. And roared.

The laugh got thinner. And the woman had trouble with her head. It flopped against her chest. Or her short brittle hair wd jam against my face, pushing that monstrous smell of old wood into my life. Old wood and wine. What there is of a slum. Of dead minds, dead fingers flapping empty in inhuman cold.

I winced (because I thot myself elegant. A fop, I'd become, and made a sign to Calvin in the mirror that the woman smelled. He grinned and rubbed his hands to steady them.

Hideous magician! The car rolled its banging stones against the dark. Ugly fiend screaming in the fire boiling your bones. Your cock, cunt, whatever in your head you think to be, is burning. Tied against a rock, straw packed tight into your eyes. POUR GASOLINE, SPREAD IT ON HIS TONGUE. NOW LIGHT THE STINKING MESS.

* * *

Shadow of a man. (Tied in a ditch, my own flesh burning in my nostrils. My body goes, simple death, but what of my mind? Who created me to this pain?)

Oh, the barns of lead are gold. You have abandoned God.

Now, he abandons you! Your brain runs like liquid in the grass.

* * *

I began to act. First hands dropped on the wino's knee. And she flopped her head spreading that rancid breath. So I pulled her head back against the seat, and moved my fingers hard against her flesh. Tugged at the wool skirt and pushed my hand between the stocking and the bumps upon her skin. Her mouth opened and she sounded like humming. Also, a shiver, like winter, went thru her/and I almost took my hands away.

Donald saw me, and when I looked across at him he felt her too. The others in front gabbled & kept informed by craning in their seats.

I moved my fingers harder, pushing the cloth up high until I saw what I thot was her underwear. Some other color than pink, with dark stains around the part that fit against her crotch.

Her head slumped forward but the eyes had opened, and there was a look in them made me look out the window. But I never moved my hands. (Someone giggled up front.)

The car moved at a steady rate. The dim lights on. Up out of East Orange and into dark Montclair. With larger whiter homes. Some dirt along the way, which meant to us, who knew only cement, some kind of tortured wealth. We wd all live up here some way. Big dogs barked at the car from driveways and Sanchez looked over his shoulder at me to get his signals straight.

Donald said something to me across the woman and she raised her head, glaring at Calvin's back.

"What the hells goin on?" Calvin laughed. I moved my fingers swifter straining for the top of the pants. Donald simply rolled her stockings down. And the woman grabbed his hand, quietly at first. But when she sensed that we would pile on her in the car shoving our tender unwashed selves in her eyes and mouth, she squeezed Donald's hand so hard it hurt.

"Bitch!"

"What're you boys tryina do?" No answer from us. The front

riders sat tight in their seats, watching the big houses, and wishing probably it was now, when they are sitting prying the dark with staler eyes.

(In those same houses, waiting until I die when they can tell all these things with proper reverence to my widow.)

* *

The woman changed her mind. (She saw what was happening and stared at me for seconds before she spoke again. She braced herself against the seat and made a weeping sound.)

"Oh my life is so fucked up. So wasted and shitty. You boys don't know. How life is. How it takes you down. You don't know . . . Those ties and shirts . . . Shit . . . how hard a woman's life can be."

Her voice got softer or she thot she'd make it tender. It came out almost bleaker than a whine. . . .

"I'm sick too. A long time. The kind of thing makes men hate you. Those sores on my self."

(She meant her vagina.)

This was news to everyone. "I'm sick," she moaned again, making her voice almost loud. "And you boys can ketch it . . . everyone'a you, get it, and scratch these bleeding sores."

Donald moved his hand away. The woman screeched now, not loud, but dragging in her breath.

Apprehension now. As if the wall was almost down but the enemy's hero arrived to pour boiling oil in my warriors' eyes. I wdn't have that easy copout. Fuck that . . . goddamit, no pleas.

I made Donald put his hands back. I scowled the way I can with one side of my mouth, the other pushing the woman back. "Shit, I don't believe that bullshit! Prove it, baby, lemme see! I wanna see the sores . . . see what they look like!"

New life now. Reinforced, the others laughed. I pushed again. "O.K., mama, runout them sores . . . lemme suck'em till they get well." Another score: but how long, we were deep in Montclair, and some car full of negroes up there wd be spotted by the police . . . that swung thru my mind and I looked up quickly thru my window. Even rolled it down to hear.

"I'm sick . . . and you boys ketch what I got you'll never have no kids. Nobody'll marry you. That's why I'ma drunk whore fallin in the streets."

Marriage,   children. What else could she burn? Donald fell away again. The rest swallowed, or moved their hands. Only Calvin ran to my aid. He grabbed a huge hunting knife still in its scabbard and twisted suddenly in his seat waving it in the woman's face. But the absurdity of it killed the move completely and we broke running down the slope:

"Shutup bitch" (Calvin) "Shutup . . . I'm a goddam policemen (sic) and we're (sic) lookin for people like you to lock'umup!"

He waved the knife and Leon even laughed at him. It was over. The woman probably knew but took it further. She screamed as loud as she could. She screamed, and screamed, her voice almost shearing off our tender heads. The scream of an actual damned soul. The actual prisoner of the world.

"SHEEEEEET, YOU BASTARDS LEMME GO.
SHEEEET. HAALP. AGGGHEEE"

Donald reached across the whore and pushed the door open. The car still moving about 20 miles an hour and the sudden air opened my eyes in the smoke. The bitch screamed and we all knew Montclair was like a beautifully furnished room and someone would hear and we would die in jail, dead niggers who couldn't be invited to parties.

Calvin reached across the seat, and shouted in my face. "Kick the bitch out!" I couldn't move. My fingers were still on her knee. The plan still fixed in my mind. But the physical world rushed thru like dirty thundering water thru a dam. They ran on me.

"Throw this dumb bitch out." Calvin grabbed her by the arm and Donald heaved against her ass. The woman tumbled over my knees and rolled, I thought, slow motion out the car. She smashed against the pavement and wobbled on her stomach hard against the curb.

The door still swung open and I moved almost without knowing thru it to bring the woman back. The smoke had blown away. I saw her body like on a white porcelain table dead with eyes rolled back. I had to get her.

I dove for the door, even as Sanchez

made the car speed up, and slammed right into the flopping steel. It hit me in the head and Leon wrenched me back against the seat. Calvin closed the door.

                      I could see the woman squatting in the street, under the fake gasoline lamp as we turned the corner, everybody screaming in the car, some insane allegiance to me.

6. The Heretics

"The whole of lower Hell is surrounded by a great wall, which is defended by rebel angels and immediately within which are punished the arch-heretics and their followers."

And then, the city of Dis, "the stronghold of Satan, named after him, . . . the deeper Hell of willful sin."

Blonde summer in our south. Always it floats down & hooks in the broad leaves of those unnamed sinister southern trees. Blonde. Yellow, a narrow sluggish water full of lives. Desires. The crimson heavy blood of a race, concealed in those absolute black nights. As if, each tiny tragedy had its own universe / or God to strike it down.

* *

Faceless slow movement. It was warm & this other guy had his sleeves rolled up. (You cd go to jail for that without any trouble. But we were loose, & maybe drunk. And I turned away & doubled up like rubber or black figure sliding at the bottom of any ocean. Thomas, Joyce, Eliot, Pound, all gone by & I thot agony at how beautiful I was. And sat sad many times in latrines fingering my joint.

But it was dusty. And time sat where it could, covered me dead, like under a stone for years, and my life was already over. A dead man stretched & a rock rolled over . . . till a light struck me straight on & I entered some madness, some hideous elegance . . . "A Patrician I wrote to him. Am I a Patrician?"

*   *

We both wore wings. My hat dipped & shoes maybe shined. This other guy was what cd happen in this country. Black & his silver wings & tilted blue cap made up for his mother's hundred bogus kids. Lynchings. And he waved his own flag in this mosquito air, and walked straight & beauty was fine, and so easy.

He didn't know who I was, or even what. The light, then (what george spoke of in his letters . . . "a soft intense light") was spread thin over the whole element of my world.

Two flyers, is what we thot people had to say. (I was a gunner, the other guy, some kind of airborne medic.) The bright wings & starched uniform. Plus, 24 dollars in my wallet.

That air rides you down, gets inside & leaves you weightless, sweating & longing for cool evening. The smells there wide & blue like eyes. And like kids, or the radio calling saturdays of the world of simple adventure. Made me weep with excitement. Heart pumping: not at all toward where we were. But the general sweep of my blood brought whole existences fresh and tingling into those images of romance had trapped me years ago.

* *

The place used me. Its softness, and in a way, indirect warmth, coming from the same twisting streets we walked. (After the bus, into the main fashion of the city: Shreveport, Louisiana. And it all erected itself for whoever . . . me, I supposed then, "it's here, and of course, the air, for my own weakness. Books fell by. But open yr eyes, nose, speak to whom you want to. Are you contemporary?")

And it seemed a world for aztecs lost on the bone side of mountains. A world, even strange, sat in that leavening light & we had come in raw from the elements. From the cardboard moonless world of ourselves . . . to whatever. To grasp at straws. (If indeed we wd confront us with those wiser selves . . . But that was blocked. The weather held. No rain. That smell wrapped me up finally & sent me off to seek its source. And men stopped us. Split our melting fingers. The sun moved till it stopped at the edge of the city. The south stretched past any eye. Outside any peculiar thot. Itself, whatever it becomes, is lost to what formal selves we have. Lust, a condition of the weather. The air, lascivious. Men die from anything . . . and this portion of my life was carefully examining the rules. How to die? How to die?

*

The place, they told us, we'd have to go to "ball" was called by them *Bottom*. The Bottom; where the colored lived. There, in whatever wordless energies your lives cd be taken up. Step back: to the edge, soothed the wind drops. Fingers are cool. Air sweeps. Trees one hundred feet down, smoothed over, the wind sways.

And

they tell me there is one place/

for me to be. Where
it all
comes down. &
you take up
your sorrowful
life. There/
with us all. To
whatever death

*

The Bottom lay like a man under a huge mountain. You cd see it slow in some mist, miles off. On the bus, the other guy craned & pulled my arm from the backseats at the mile descent we'd make to get the juice. The night had it. Air like mild seasons and come. That simple elegance of semen on the single buds of air. As if the night were feathers . . . and they settled solid on my speech . . . and preached sinister love for the sun.

The day . . . where had it gone? It had moved

away as we wound down into the mass of trees and broken lives.

The bus stopped finally a third of the way down the slope. The last whites had gotten off a mile back & 6 or seven negroes and we two flyers had the bus. The driver smiled his considerate paternal smile in the mirror at our heads as we popped off. Whole civilization considered, considered. "They live in blackness. No thought runs out. They kill each other & hate the sun. They have no God save who they are. Their black selves. Their lust. Their insensible animal eyes."

"Hey, son, 'dyou pay for him?" He asked me because I hopped off last. He meant not my friend, the other pilot, but some slick head coon in yellow pants cooling it at top speed into the grass. & knowing no bus driver was running in after no 8 cents.

> "Man, the knives
> flash. Souls
> are spittle
> on black earth. Metal
> dug in flesh chipping
> at the bone."

I turned completely around to look at the bus driver. I saw a knife in him hacking chunks of bone. He stared, & smiled at the thin mob rolling down the hill. Friday night. Nigguhs is Nigguhs. I agreed. & smiled, he liked the wings, had a son who flew. "You gon pay for that ol coon?"

"No," I said, "No. Fuck, man, I hate coons." He laughed. I saw the night around his head warped with blood. The bus, moon & trees floated heavily in blood. It washed down the side of the hill & the negroes ran from it.

I turned toward my friend who was loping down the hill shouting at me & ran toward him & what we saw at the foot of the hill. The man backed the bus up & turned around / pretending he was a mystic.

*　*　*

I caught Don(?) and walked beside him laughing. And the trees passed & some lights and houses sat just in front of us. We trailed the rest of the crowd & they spread out soon & disappeared into their lives.

The Bottom was like Spruce & Belmont (the ward) in Nwk. A culture of violence and foodsmells. There, for me. Again. And it stood strange when I thot finally how much irony. I had gotten so elegant (that was college / a new order of foppery). But then the army came & I was dragged into a kind of stillness. Everything I learned stacked up and the bones of love shattered in my face. And I never smiled again at anything. Everything casual in my life (except that life itself) was gone. Those naked shadows of men against the ruined walls. Penis, testicles. All there (and I sat burned like wire, w/ farmers, thinking of what I had myself. When I peed I thot that. "Look. Look what you're using to do this. A dick. And two balls, one a little lower than the other. The first thing warped & crooked when it hardened." But it meant nothing. The books meant nothing. My idea was to be loved. What I accused John of. And it meant going into that huge city melting. And the first face I saw I went to and we went home and he shoved his old empty sack of self against my frozen skin.

*   *

Shadows, phantoms, recalled by that night. Its heavy moon. A turning slow and dug in the flesh and wet spots grew under my khaki arms. Alive to mystery. And the horror in my eyes made them large and the moon came in. The moon and the quiet southern night.

*   *

We passed white shut houses. It seemed misty or smoky. Things settled dumbly in the fog and we passed, our lives spinning off in simple anonymous laughter.

We were walking single file because of the dirt road. Not wanting to get in the road where drunk niggers roared by in dead autos stabbing each others' laughter in some gray abandon of suffering. That they suffered and cdn't know it. Knew that somehow, forever. Each dead nigger stinking his same suffering thru us. Each word of blues some dead face melting. Some life drained off in silence. Under some gray night of smoke. They roared thru this night screaming. Heritage of hysteria and madness, the old meat smells and silent gray sidewalks of the North. Each father, smiling mother, walked thru these nights frightened of their children. Of the white sun scalding their nights. Of each hollow loud footstep in whatever abstruse hall.

* * *

THE JOINT

(a letter was broken and I can't remember. The other guy laughed, at the name. And patted his. I took it literal and looked thru my wallet as not to get inflamed and sink on that man screaming of my new loves. My cold sin in the cities. My fear of my own death's insanity, and an actual longing for men that brooded in each finger of my memory.

He laughed at the sign. And we stood, for the moment (he made me warm with his laughing), huge white men who knew the world (our wings) and would give it to whoever showed as beautiful or in our sad lone smiles, at least willing to love us.

He pointed, like Odysseus wd. Like Virgil, the weary shade, at some circle. For Dante, me, the yng wild virgin of the universe to look. To see what terror. What illusion. What sudden shame, the world is made. Of what death and lust I fondled and thot to make beautiful or escape, at least, into some other light, where each death was abstract & intimate.

* * * *

There were, I think, 4

women standing across the street. The neon winked, and the place seemed mad to be squatted in this actual wilderness. "For Madmen Only." Mozart's Ornithology and yellow greasy fags moaning german jazz. Already, outside. The passage, I sensed in those women. And black space yawned. Damned and burning souls. What has been your sin? Your ugliness?

And they waved. Calling us natural names. "Hey, ol bigeye sweet nigger . . . com'ere." "Littl ol' skeeter dick . . . don't you want none?" And to each other giggling at their centuries, "Um, that big nigger look sweet" . . . "Yeh, that little one look sweet too." The four walls of some awesome city. Once past you knew that your life had ended. That roads took up the other side, and wound into thicker dusk. Darker, more insane, nights.

And Don shouted back, convinced of his hugeness, his grace . . . my wisdom. I shuddered at their eyes and tried to draw back into the shadows. He grabbed my arm, and laughed at my dry lips.

Of the 4, the pretty one was Della and the fat one, Peaches. 17 year old whores strapped to negro weekends. To the black thick earth and smoke it made to hide their maudlin sins. I stared and was silent and they, the girls and Don, the white man, laughed at my whispering and sudden midnight world.
Frightened of myself, of the night's talk, and not of them. Of myself.

The other two girls fell away hissing at their poverty. And the two who had caught us exchanged strange jokes.

Told us of themselves thru the other's mouth. Don already clutching the thin beautiful Della. A small tender flower she seemed. Covered with the pollen of desire. Ignorance. Fear of what she was. At her 17th birthday she had told us she wept, in the department store, at her death. That the years wd make her old and her dresses wd get bigger. She laughed and felt my arm, and laughed, Don pulling her closer. And ugly negroes passed close to us frowning at the uniforms and my shy clipped speech which they called "norf."

So Peaches was mine. Fat with short baked hair split at the ends. Pregnant empty stomach. Thin shrieky voice like knives against a blackboard. Speeded up records. Big feet in white, shiny polished shoes. Fat tiny hands full of rings. A purple dress with wrinkles across the stomach. And perspiring flesh that made my khakis wet.

The four of us went in the joint and the girls made noise to show this world their craft. The two rich boys from the castle. (Don looked at me to know how much cash I had and shouted and shook his head and called "18, man," patting his ass.)

The place was filled with shades. Ghosts. And the huge ugly hands of actual spooks. Standing around the bar, spilling wine on greasy shirts. Yelling at a fat yellow spliv who talked about all their mothers, pulling out their drinks. Laughing with wet cigarettes and the paper stuck to fat lips. Crazy as anything in the world, and sad because of it. Yelling as not to hear the sad breathing world. Turning all music up. Screaming all lyrics. Tough black men . . . weak black men. Filthy drunk women whose perfume was cheap unnatural flowers. Quiet thin ladies whose lives had ended and whose teeth hung stupidly in their silent mouths . . . rotted by thousands of nickel wines. A smell of despair and drunkenness. Silence and laughter, and the sounds of their movement under it. Their frightening lives.

* *

Of course the men didn't dig the two imitation white boys come in on their leisure. And when I spoke someone wd turn and stare, or laugh, and point me out. The quick new jersey speech, full of italian idiom, and the invention of the jews. Quick to describe. Quicker to condemn. And when we finally got a seat in the back of the place, where the dance floor was, the whole place had turned a little to look. And the girls ate it all up, laughing as loud as their vanity permitted. Other whores grimaced and talked almost as loud . . . putting us all down.

10 feet up on the wall, in a kind of balcony, a jew sat, with thick glasses and a cap, in front of a table. He had checks and money at the table & where the winding steps went up to him a line of shouting woogies waved their pay & waited for that bogus christ to give them the currency of that place. Two tremendous muthafuckers with stale white teeth grinned in back of the jew and sat with baseball bats to protect the western world.

On the dance floor people hung on each other. Clutched their separate flesh and thought, my god, their separate thots. They stunk. They screamed. They moved hard against each other. They pushed. And wiggled to keep the music on. Two juke boxes blasting from each corner, and four guys on a bandstand who had taken off their stocking caps and come to the place with guitars. One with a saxophone. All that screaming came together with the smells and the music, the people bumped their asses and squeezed their eyes shut.

Don ordered a bottle of schenley's which cost 6 dollars for a pint after hours. And Peaches grabbed my arm and led me to the floor.

The dancing like a rite no one knew, or had use for outside their secret lives. The flesh they felt when they moved, or I felt all their flesh and was happy and drunk and looked at the black faces knowing all the world thot they were my own, and lusted at that anonymous America I broke out of, and long for it now, where I am.

We danced, this face and I, close so I had her sweat in my mouth, her flesh the only sound my brain could use. Stinking, and the music over us like a sky, choked any other movement off. I danced. And my history was there, had passed no further. Where it ended, here, the light white talking jig, died in the arms of some sentry of Africa. Some short-haired witch out of my mother's most hideous dreams. I was nobody now, mama. Nobody. Another secret nigger. No one the white world wanted or would look at. (My mother shot herself. My father killed by a white tree fell on him. The sun, now, smothered. Dead.

* * *

Don and his property had gone when we finished. 3 or 4 dances later. My uniform dripping and soggy on my skin. My hands wet. My eyes turned up to darkness. Only my nerves sat naked and my ears were stuffed with gleaming horns. No one face sat alone, just that image of myself, forever screaming. Chiding me. And the girl, peaches, laughed louder than the crowd. And wearily I pushed her hand from my fly and looked for a chair.

We sat at the table and I looked around the room for my brother, and only shapes of black men moved by. Their noise and smell. Their narrow paths to death. I wanted to panic, but the dancing and gin had me calm, almost cruel in what I saw.

Peaches talked. She talked at what she thought she saw. I slumped on the table and we emptied another pint. My stomach turning rapidly and the room moved without me. And I slapped my hands on the table laughing at myself. Peaches laughed, peed, thinking me crazy, returned, laughed again. I was silent now, and felt the drunk and knew I'd go out soon. I got up feeling my legs, staring at the fat guard with me, and made to leave. I mumbled at her. Something ugly. She laughed and held me up. Holding me from the door. I smiled casual, said, "Well, honey, I gotta split . . . I'm fucked up." She grinned the same casual, said, "You can't go now, big eye, we jist gittin into sumpum."

"Yeh, yeh, I know . . . but I can't make it." My head was shaking on my chest, fingers stabbed in my pockets. I staggered like an acrobat toward the stars and trees I saw at one end of the hall. "UhUh . . . baby where you goin?"

"Gotta split, gotta split . . . really, baby, I'm fucked . . . up." And I twisted my arm away, moving faster as I knew I should toward the vague smell of air. Peaches was laughing and tugging a little at my sleeve. She came around and rubbed my tiny pecker with her fingers. And still I moved away. She had my elbow when I reached the road, head still slumped, and feet pushing for a space to go down solid on. When I got outside she moved in front of me. Her other girls had moved in too, to see what was going on. Why Peaches had to relinquish her share so soon. I saw the look she gave me and wanted somehow to protest, say, "I'm sorry. I'm fucked up. My mind, is screwy, I don't know why. I can't think. I'm sick. I've been fucked in the ass. I love books and smells and my own voice. You don't want me. Please, Please, don't want me."

But she didn't see. She heard, I guess, her own blood. Her own whore's bones telling her what to do. And I twisted away from her, headed across the road and into the dark. Out of, I hoped, Bottom, toward what I thot was light. And I could hear the girls laughing at me, at Peaches, at whatever thing I'd brought to them to see.

So the fat bitch grabbed my hat. A blue "overseas cap" they called it in the service. A cunt cap the white boys called it. Peaches had it and was laughing like kids in the playground doing the same thing to some unfortunate fag. I knew the second she got it, and stared crazily at her, and my look softened to fear and I grinned, I think. "You ain't going back without dis cap, big eye nigger," tossing it over my arms to her screaming friends. They tossed it back to her. I stood in the center staring at the lights. Listening to my own head. The things I wanted. Who I thot I was. What was it? Why was this going on? Who was involved? I screamed for the hat. And they shot up the street, 4 whores, Peaches last in her fat, shouting at them to throw the hat to her. I stood for a while and then tried to run after them. I cdn't go back to my base without that cap. Go to jail, drunken nigger! Throw him in the stockade! You're out of uniform, shine! When I got close to them, the other three ran off, and only Peaches stood at the top of the hill waving the hat at me, cackling at her wealth. And she screamed at the world, that she'd won some small niche in it. And did a dance, throwing her big hips at me, cursing and spitting . . . laughing at the drunk who had sat down on the curb and started to weep and plead at her for some cheap piece of cloth.

And I was mumbling under the tears. "My hat, please, my hat. I gotta get back, please." But she came over to me and leaned on my shoulder, brushing the cap in my face. "You gonna buy me another drink . . . just one more?"

* * *

She'd put the cap in her brassiere, and told me about the Cotton Club. Another place at the outskirts of Bottom. And we went there, she was bouncing and had my hand, like a limp cloth. She talked of her life. Her husband, in the service too. Her family. Her friends. And predicted I would be a lawyer or something else rich.

The Cotton Club, was in a kind of ditch. Or valley. Or three flights down. Or someplace removed from where we stood. Like movies, or things you think up abstractly. Poles, where the moon was. Signs, for streets, beers, pancakes. Out front. No one moved outside, it was too late. Only whores and ignorant punks were out.

The place when we got in was all light. A bar. Smaller than the joint, with less people and quieter. Tables were strewn around and there was a bar with a fat white man sitting on a stool behind it. His elbows rested on the bar and he chewed a cigar spitting the flakes on the floor. He smiled at Peaches, knowing her, leaning from his talk. Four or five stood at the bar. White and black, moaning and drunk. And I wondered how it was they got in. The both colors? And I saw a white stripe up the center of the floor, and taped to the bar, going clear up, over the counter. And the black man who talked, stood at one side, the left, of the tape, further-est from the door. And the white man, on the right, closest to the door. They talked, and were old friends, touching each other, and screaming with laughter at what they said.

We got vodka. And my head slumped, but I looked around to see, what place this was. Why they moved. Who was dead. What faces came. What moved. And they sat in their various skins and stared at me.

Empty man. Walk thru shadows. All lives the same.

They give you wishes. The old people at the window. Dead man. Rised, come gory to their side. Wish to be lovely, to be some other self. Even here, without you. Some other soul, than the filth I feel. Have in me. Guilt, like something of God's. Some separate suffering self.

Locked in a lightless shaft. Light at the top, pure white sun. And shadows twist my voice. Iron clothes to suffer. To pull down, what had grown so huge. My life wrested away. The old wood. Eyes of the damned uncomprehending. Who it was. Old slack nigger. Drunk punk. Fag. Get up. Where's your home? Your mother. Rich nigger. Porch sitter. It comes down. So cute, huh? Yellow thing. Think you cute.

And suffer so slight, in the world. The world? Literate? Brown skinned. Stuck in the ass. Suffering from what? Can you read? Who is T. S. Eliot? So what? A cross. You've got to like girls. Weirdo. Break, Roi, break. Now come back, do it again. Get down, hard. Come up. Keep your legs high, crouch hard when you get the ball . . . churn, churn, churn. A blue jacket, and alone. Where? A chinese restaurant. Talk to me. Goddamnit. Say something. You never talk, just sit there, impossible to love. Say something. Alone, there, under those buildings. Your shadows. Your selfish tongue. Move. Frightened bastard. Frightened scared sissy motherfucker.

* * *

I felt my head go down. And I moved my hand to keep

it up. Peaches laughed again. The white man turned and clicked his tongue at her wagging his hand. I sucked my thin mustache, scratched my chest, held my sore head dreamily. Peaches laughed. 2 bottles more of vodka she drank (half pints at 3.00 each) & led me out the back thru some dark alley down steps and thru a dark low hall to where she lived.

She was dragging me, I tried to walk and couldn't and stuck my hands in my pockets to keep them out of her way. Her house, a room painted blue and pink with Rheingold women glued to the wall. Calendars. The Rotogravure. The picture of her husband? Who she thot was some officer, and he was grinning like watermelon photos with a big white apron on and uncle jemima white hat and should've had a skillet. I slumped on the bed, and she made me get up and sit in a chair and she took my hat out of her clothes and threw it across the room. Coffee, she said, you want coffee. She brought it anyway, and I got some in my mouth. Like winter inside me. I coughed and she laughed. I turned my head away from the bare bulb. And she went in a closet and got out a thin yellow cardboard shade and stuck it on the light trying to push the burned part away from the huge white bulb.

Willful sin. in your toilets jerking off. You refused God. All frauds, the cold mosques glitter winters. "Morsh-Americans." Infidels fat niggers at the gates. What you want. What you are now. Liar. All sins, against your God. Your own flesh. TALK. TALK.

And I still slumped and she pushed my head back against the greasy seat and sat on my lap grinning in my ear, asking me to say words that made her laugh. Orange. Probably. Girl. Newark. Peaches. Talk like a white man, she laughed. From up north (she made the "th" an "f").

And sleep seemed good to me. Something my mother would say. My grandmother, all those heads of heaven. To get me in. Roi, go to sleep, You need sleep, and eat more. You're too skinny. But this fat bitch pinched my neck and my eyes would shoot open and my hands dropped touching the linoleum and I watched roaches, trying to count them getting up to 5, and slumped again. She pinched me. And I made some move and pushed myself up standing and went to the sink and stuck my head in cold water an inch above the pile of stale egg dishes floating in brown she used to wash the eggs off.

I shook my head. Took out my handkerchief to dry my hands, leaving my face wet and cold, for a few seconds. But the heat came back, and I kept pulling my shirt away from my body and smelled under my arms, trying to laugh with Peaches, who was laughing again.

I wanted to talk now. What to say. About my life. My thots. What I'd found out, and tried to use. Who I was. For her. This lady, with me.

She pushed me backward on the bed

and said you're sleepy I'll get in with you. and I rolled on my side trying to push up on the bed and couldn't, and she pulled one of my shoes off and put it in her closet. I turned on my back and groaned at my head told her again I had to go. I was awol or something. I had to explain awol and she knew what it meant when I finished. Everybody that she knew was that. She was laughing again. O, God, I wanted to shout and it was groaned. Oh, God.

She had my pants in her fingers pulling them over my one shoe. I was going to pull them back up and they slipped from my hands and I tried to raise up and she pushed me back. "Look, Ol nigger, I ain't even gonna charge you. I like you." And my head was turning, flopping straight back on the chenille, and the white ladies on the wall did tricks and grinned and pissed on the floor. "Baby, look, Baby," I was sad because I fell. From where it was I'd come to. My silence. The streets I used for books. All come in. Lost. Burned. And soothing she rubbed her hard hair on my stomach and I meant to look to see if grease was there it was something funny I meant to say, but my head twisted to the side and I bit the chenille and figured there would be a war or the walls would collapse and I would have to take the black girl out, a hero. And my mother would grin and tell her friends and my father would call me "mcgee" and want me to tell about it.

When I had only my shorts on she pulled her purple dress over her head. It was all she had, except a gray brassiere with black wet moons where her arms went down. She kept it on.

Some light got in from a window. And one white shadow sat on a half-naked woman on the wall. Nothing else moved. I drew my legs up tight & shivered. Her hands pulled me to her.

*

It was Chicago. The fags & winter. Sick thin boy, come out of those els. Ask about the books. Thin mathematics and soup. Not the black Beverly, but here for the first time I'd seen it. Been pushed in. What was flesh I hadn't used till then. To go back. To sit lonely. Need to be used, touched, and see for the first time how it moved. Why the world moved on it. Not a childish sun. A secret fruit. But hard things between their legs. And lives governed under it. So here, it can sit now, as evil. As demanding, for me, to have come thru and found it again. I hate it. I hate to touch you. To feel myself go soft and want some person not myself. And here, it had moved outside. Left my wet fingers and was not something I fixed. But dropped on me and sucked me inside. That I walked the streets hunting for warmth. To be pushed under a quilt, and call it love. To shit water for days and say I've been loved. Been warm. A real thing in the world. See my shadow. My reflection. I'm here, alive. Touch me. Please. Please, touch me.

* * *

She rolled on me and after my pants were off pulled me on her thick stomach. I dropped between her legs and she felt between my cheeks to touch my balls. Her fingers were warm and she grabbed everything in her palm and wanted them harder. She pulled to get them harder and it hurt me. My head hurt me. My life. And she pulled, breathing spit on my chest. "Comeon, Baby, Comeon . . . Get hard." It was like being slapped. And she did it that way, trying to laugh. "Get hard . . . Get hard." And nothing happened or the light changed and I couldn't see the paper woman.

And she slapped me now, with her hand. A short hard punch and my head spun. She cursed. & she pulled as hard as she could. I was going to be silent but she punched again and I wanted to laugh . . . it was another groan. "Young peachtree," she had her mouth at my ear lobe. "You don't like women, huh?" "No wonder you so pretty . . . ol bigeye faggot." My head was turned from that side to the other side turned to the other side turned again and had things in it bouncing.

"How'd you ever get in them airplanes, peaches (her name she called me)? Why they let fairies in there now? (She was pulling too hard now & I thot everything would give and a hole in my stomach would let out words and tears.) Goddam punk, you gonna fuck me tonight or I'm gonna pull your fuckin dick aloose."

How to be in this world. How to be here, not a shadow, but thick bone and meat. Real flesh under real sun. And real tears falling on black sweet earth.

I was crying now. Hot hot tears and trying to sing. Or say to Peaches. "Please, you don't know me. Not what's in my head. I'm beautiful. Stephen Dedalus. A mind, here where there is only steel. Nothing else. Young pharaoh under trees. Young pharaoh, romantic, liar. Feel my face, how tender. My eyes. My soul is white, pure white, and soars. Is the God himself. This world and all others.

And I thot of a black man under the el who took me home in the cold. And I remembered telling him all these things. And how he listened and showed me his new suit. And I crawled out of bed morning and walked thru the park for my train. Loved. Afraid. Huger than any world. And the hot tears wet Peaches and her bed and she slapped me for pissing.

I rolled hard on her and stuck my soft self between her thighs. And ground until I felt it slip into her stomach. And it got harder in her spreading the meat. Her arms around my hips pulled down hard and legs locked me and she started yelling. Faggot. Faggot. Sissy Motherfucker. And I pumped myself. Straining. Threw my hips at her. And she yelled, for me to fuck her. Fuck her. Fuck me, you lousy fag. And I twisted, spitting tears, and hitting my hips on hers, pounding flesh in her, hearing myself weep.

* * * * * * * *

Later, I slipped out into Bottom. Without my hat or tie,

shoes loose and pants wrinkled and filthy. No one was on the streets now. Not even the whores. I walked not knowing where I was or was headed for. I wanted to get out. To see my parents, or be silent for the rest of my life. Huge moon was my light. Black straight trees the moon showed. And the dirt roads and scattered wreck houses. I still had money and I.D., and a pack of cigarettes. I trotted, then stopped, then trotted, and talked outloud to myself. And laughed a few times. The place was so still, so black and full of violence. I felt myself.

At one road, there were several houses. Larger than a lot of them. Porches, yards. All of them sat on cinder blocks so the vermin would have trouble getting in. Someone called to me. I thought it was in my head and kept moving, but slower. They called again. "Hey, psst. Hey comere." A whisper, but loud. "Comere, baby." All the sides of the houses were lit up but underneath, the space the cinder blocks made was black. And the moon made a head shadow on the ground, and I could see an arm in the same light. Someone kneeling under one of the houses, or an arm and the shadow of a head. I stood straight, and stiff, and tried to see right thru the dark. The voice came back, chiding like. Something you want. Whoever wants. That we do and I wondered who it was kneeling in the dark, at the end of the world, and I heard breathing when I did move, hard and closed.

I bent toward the space to see who it was. Why they had called. And I saw it was a man. Round red-rimmed eyes, sand-colored jew hair, and teeth for a face. He had been completely under the house but when I came he crawled out and I saw his dripping smile and yellow soggy skin full of red freckles. He said, "Come on here. Comere a second." I moved to turn away. The face like a dull engine. Eyes blinking. When I turned he reached for my arm grazing my shirt and the voice could be flushed down a toilet. He grinned and wanted to panic seeing me move. "Lemme suck yo dick, honey. Huh?" I was backing away like from the hyena cage to see the rest of them. Baboons? Or stop at the hotdog stand and read a comic book. He came up off all fours and sat on his knees and toes, shaking his head and hips. "Comeon baby, comeon now." As I moved back he began to scream at me. All lust, all panic, all silence and sorrow, and finally when I had moved and was trotting down the road, I looked around and he was standing up with his hands cupped to his mouth yelling into the darkness in complete hatred of what was only some wraith. Irreligious spirit pushing thru shadows, frustrating and confusing the flesh. He screamed behind me and when the moon sunk for minutes behind the clouds or trees his scream was like some animal's, some hurt ugly thing dying alone.

* * * *

It was good to run. I would jump every few steps like hurdling, and shoot my arm out straight to take it right, landing on my right heel, snapping the left leg turned and flat, bent for the next piece. 3 steps between 180 yard lows,

7 or 9 between the 220's. The 180's I thought the most beautiful. After the first one, hard on the heel and springing up. Like music; a scale. Hit, 1–23. UP (straight right leg, down low just above the wood. Left turned at the angle, flat, tucked. Head low to the knee, arms reaching for the right toe, pulling the left leg to snap it down. HIT (right foot). Snap left HIT (left). Stride. The big one. 1–23. UP. STRETCH. My stride was long enough for the 3 step move. Stretching and hopping almost but in perfect scale. And I moved ahead of Wang and held it, the jew boy pooping at the last wood. I hit hard and threw my chest out, pulling the knees high, under my chin. Arms pushing. The last ten yards I picked up 3 and won by that, head back wrong (Nap said) and galloping like a horse (wrong again Nap said) but winning in new time and leaping in the air like I saw heroes do in flicks.

* * * *

I got back to where I thought the Joint would be, and there were city-like houses and it was there somewhere. From there, I thought I could walk out, get back to the world. It was getting blue again. Sky lightening blue and gray trees and buildings black against it. And a few lights going on in some wood houses. A few going off. There were alleys now. And high wood fences with slats missing. Dogs walked across the road. Cats sat on the fences watching. Dead cars sulked. Old newspapers torn in half pushed against fire hydrants or stoops and made tiny noises flapping if the wind came up.

I had my hands in my pockets, relaxed. The anonymous seer again. Looking slowly at things. Touching wood rails so years later I would remember I had touched wood rails in Louisiana when no one watched. Swinging my leg at cans, talking to the cats, doing made up dance steps or shadow boxing. And I came to a corner & saw some big black soldier stretched in the road with blood falling out of his head and stomach. I thot first it was Don. But this guy was too big and was in the infantry. I saw a paratrooper patch on his cap which was an inch away from his chopped up face, but the blue and silver badge had been taken off his shirt.

He was groaning quiet, talking to himself. Not dead, but almost. And I bent over him to ask what happened. He couldn't open his eyes and didn't hear me anyway. Just moaned and moaned losing his life on the ground. I stood up and wondered what to do. And looked at the guy and saw myself and looked over my shoulder when I heard someone move behind me. A tall black skinny woman hustled out of the shadows and looking back at me disappeared into a hallway. I shouted after her. And stepped in the street to see the door she'd gone in.

I turned to go back to the soldier and there was a car pulling up the road. A red swiveling light on top and cops inside. One had his head hung out the window and yelled toward me. "Hey, you, Nigger, What's goin on?" That would be it. AWOL. Out of uniform (with a norfern accent). Now murder too. "30 days for nigger killing." I spun and moved. Down the road & they started to turn.

I hit the fence, swinging up and dove into the black yard beyond. Fell on my hands and knees & staggered, got up, tripped on garbage, got up, swinging my hands, head down and charged off in the darkness.

The crackers were yelling on the other side of the fence and I could hear one trying to scale it. There was another fence beyond, and I took it the same as the first. Swinging down into another yard. And turned right and went over another fence, ripping my shirt. Huge cats leaped out of my path and lights went on in some houses. I saw the old woman who'd been hiding near the soldier just as I got to the top of one fence. She was standing in a hallway that led out in that yard, and she ducked back laughing when she saw me. I started to go after her, but I just heaved a big rock in her direction and hit another fence.

I got back to where the city houses left off, and there were the porches and cinder blocks again. I wondered if "sweet peter eater" would show up. (He'd told me his name.) And I ran up the roads hoping it wdn't get light until I found Peaches again.

At the Cotton Club I went down the steps, thru the alley, rested in the black hall, and tapped on Peaches' door. I bounced against it with my ass, resting between bumps, and fell backward when she opened the door to shove her greasy eyes in the hall.

"You back again? What you want, honey? Know you don't want no pussy. Doyuh?"

I told her I had to stay there. That I wanted to stay there, with her. That I'd come back and wanted to sleep. And if she wanted money I'd give her some. And she grabbed my wrist and pulled me in, still bare-assed except for the filthy brassiere.

She loved me, she said. Or liked me a lot. She wanted me to stay, with her. We could live together and she would show me how to fuck. How to do it good. And we could start as soon as she took a pee. And to undress, and get in bed and wait for her, unless I wanted some coffee, which she brought back anyway and sat on the edge of the bed reading a book about Linda Darnell.

"Oh, we can have some good times baby. Movies, all them juke joints. You live here with me and I'll be good to you. Wallace (her husband) ain't due back in two years. We can raise hell waiting for him." She put the book down and scratched the inside of her thighs, then under one arm. Her hair was standing up and she went to a round mirror over the sink and brushed it. And turned around and shook her big hips at me, then pumped the air to suggest our mission. She came back and we talked about our lives: then she pushed back the sheets, helped me undress again, got me hard and pulled me into her. I came too quick and she had to twist her hips a few minutes longer to come herself. "Uhauh, good even on a sof. But I still got to teach you."

* * * * * *

I woke up about 1 the next afternoon. The sun, thru that

one window, full in my face. Hot, dust in it. But the smell was good. A daytime smell. And I heard daytime voices thru the window up and fat with optimism. I pulled my hands under my head and looked for Peaches, who was out of bed. She was at the kitchen end of the room cutting open a watermelon. She had on a slip, and no shoes, but her hair was down flat and greased so it made a thousand slippery waves ending in slick feathers at the top of her ears.

"Hello, sweet," she turned and had a huge slice of melon on a plate for me. It was bright in the room now & she'd swept and straightened most of the shabby furniture in her tiny room. And the door sat open so more light, and air could come in. And her radio up on a shelf above the bed was on low with heavy blues and twangy guitar. She sat the melon on the "end table" and moved it near the bed. She had another large piece, dark red and spilling seeds in her hand and had already started. "This is good. Watermelon's a good breakfast. Peps you up."

And I felt myself smiling, and it seemed that things had come to an order. Peaches sitting on the edge of the bed, just beginning to perspire around her forehead, eating the melon in both hands, and mine on a plate, with a fork (since I was "smart" and could be a lawyer, maybe). It seemed settled. That she was to talk softly in her vague american, and I was to listen and nod, or remark on the heat or the sweetness of the melon. And that the sun was to be hot on our faces and the day smell come in with dry smells of knuckles or greens or peas cooking somewhere. Things moving naturally for us. At what bliss we took. At our words. And slumped together in anonymous houses I thought of black men sitting on their beds this saturday of my life listening quietly to their wives' soft talk. And felt the world grow together as I hadn't known it. All lies before, I thought. All fraud and sickness. This was the world. It leaned under its own suns, and people moved on it. A real world. of flesh, of smells, of soft black harmonies and color. The dead maelstrom of my head, a sickness. The sun so warm and lovely on my face, the melon sweet going down. Peaches' music and her radio's. I cursed chicago, and softened at the world. "You look so sweet," she was saying. "Like you're real rested."

* * * * *

I dozed again even before I finished the melon and Peaches had taken it and put it in the icebox when I woke up. The greens were cooking in our house now. The knuckles on top simmering. And biscuits were cooking, and chicken. "How you feel, baby," she watched me stretch. I yawned loud and scratched my back getting up to look at what the stove was doing. "We gonna eat a good lunch before we go to the movies. You so skinny, you could use a good meal. Don't you eat nuthin?" And she put down her cooking fork and hugged me to her, the smell of her, heavy, traditional, secret.

"Now you get dressed, and go get me some tomatoes . . . so we can eat." And it was good that there was something I could do for her. And go out into that world too. Now I knew it was there. And flesh.

I put on the stained khakis & she gave me my hat. "You'll get picked up without yo cap. We have to get you some clothes so you can throw that stuff away. The army don't need you no way." She laughed. "Leastways not as much as I does. Old Henry at the joint'll give you a job. You kin count money as good as that ol' jew I bet."

And I put the tie on, making some joke, and went out shopping for my wife.

* * * * * * *

Into that sun. The day was bright and people walked by me smiling. And waved "Hey" (a greeting) and they all knew I was Peaches' man.

I got to the store and stood talking to the man about the weather about airplanes and a little bit about new jersey. He waved at me when I left "O.K. . . . you take it easy now." "O.K., I'll see you," I said. I had the tomatoes and some plums and peaches I bought too. I took a tomato out of the bag and bit the sweet flesh. Pushed my hat on the back of my head and strutted up the road toward the house.

It was a cloud I think came up. Something touched me. "That color which cowardice brought out in me." Fire burns around the tombs. Closed from the earth. A despair came down. Alien grace. Lost to myself, I'd come back. To that ugliness sat inside me waiting. And the mere sky graying could do it. Sky spread thin out away from this place. Over other heads. Beautiful unknowns. And my marriage a heavy iron to this tomb. "Show us your countenance." Your light.

It was a light clap of thunder. No lightning. And the sky grayed. Introitus. That word came in. And the yellow light burning in my rooms. To come to see the world, and yet lose it. And find sweet grace alone.

It was this or what I thought, made me turn and drop the tomatoes on Peaches' porch. Her window was open and I wondered what she was thinking. How my face looked in her head. I turned and looked at the sad bag of tomatoes. The peaches, some rolling down one stair. And a light rain came down. I walked away from the house. Up the road, to go out of Bottom.

* * * *

The rain wet my face and I wanted to cry because I thot of the huge black girl watching her biscuits get cold. And her radio playing without me. The rain was hard for a second, drenching me. And then it stopped, and just as quick the sun came out. Heavy bright hot. I trotted for a while then walked slow, measuring my steps. I stank of sweat and the uniform was a joke.

I asked some pople how to get out and they pointed up the road where 10 minutes walking had me at the bottom of the hill the bus came down. A wet wind blew up soft full of sun and I began to calm. To see what had happened. Who I was and what I thought my life should be. What people called "experience." Young male. My hands in my pockets, and the grimy silver wings still hanging gravely on my filthy shirt. The feeling in my legs was to run up the rest of the hill but I just took long strides and stretched myself and wondered if I'd have K.P. or some army chastisement for being 2 days gone.

3 tall guys were coming down the hill I didn't see until they got close enough to speak to me. One laughed (at the way I looked). Tall strong black boys with plenty of teeth and pegged rayon pants. I just looked and nodded and kept on. One guy, with an imitation tattersall vest with no shirt, told the others I was in the Joint last night "playin cool." Slick city nigger, one said. I was going to pass close to them and the guy with the vest put up his hand and asked me where I was coming from. One with suspenders and a belt asked me what the wings stood for. I told him something. The third fellow just grinned. I moved to walk around them and the fellow with the vest asked could he borrow fifty cents. I only had a dollar in my pocket and told him that. There was no place to get change. He said to give him the dollar. I couldnt do that and get back to my base I told him and wanted to walk away. And one of the guys had gotten around in back of me and kneeled down and the guy with the vest pushed me backward so I fell over the other's back. I fell backward into the dust, and my hat fell off, and I didn't think I was mad but I still said something stupid like "What'd you do that for."

"I wanna borrow a dollar, Mr. Half-white muthafucka. And that's that." I sidestepped the one with the vest and took a running step but the grinning one tripped me, and I fell tumbling head forward back in the dust. This time when they laughed I got up and spun around and hit the guy who tripped me in the face. His nose was bleeding and he was cursing while the guy with the suspenders grabbed my shoulders and held me so the hurt one could punch me back. The guy with the vest punched too. And I got in one good kick into his groin, and stomped hard on one of their feet. The tears were coming again and I was cursing, now when they hit me, completely crazy. The dark one with the suspenders punched me in my stomach and I felt sick and the guy with the vest, the last one I saw, kicked me in my hip. The guy still held on for a while then he pushed me at one of the others and they hit me as I fell. I got picked up and was screaming at them to let me go. "Bastards, you filthy stupid bastards, let me go." Crazy out of my head. Stars were out. And there were no fists just dull distant jolts that spun my head. It was in a cave this went on. With music and whores danced on the tables. I sat reading from a book aloud and they danced to my reading. When I finished reading I got up from the table and for some reason, fell forward weeping on the floor. The negroes danced around my body and spilled whisky on my clothes. I woke up 2 days later, with white men, screaming for God to help me.

SOUND AND IMAGE

What is hell? Your definitions.

I am and was and will be a social animal. Hell is definable only in those terms. I can get no place else; it wdn't exist.

Hell in this book which moves from sound and image ("association complexes") into fast narrative is what vision I had of it around 1960–61 and that fix on my life, and my interpretation of my earlier life.

Hell in the head.

The torture of being the unseen object, and, the constantly observed subject.

The flame of social dichotomy. Split open down the center, which is the early legacy of the black man unfocused on blackness. The dichotomy of what is seen and taught and desired opposed to what is felt. Finally, God, is simply a white man, a white "idea," in this society, unless we have made some other image which is stronger, and can deliver us from the salvation of our enemies.

For instance, if we can bring back on ourselves, the absolute pain our people must have felt when they came onto this shore, we are more ourselves again, and can begin to put history back in our menu, and forget the propaganda of devils that they are not devils.

*　*　*　*

Hell is actual, and people with hell in their heads. But the pastoral moments in a man's life will also mean a great deal as far as his emotional references. One thinks of home, or the other "homes" we have had. And we remember w/ love those things bathed in soft black light. The struggles away or toward this peace is Hell's function. (Wars of consciousness. Antithetical definitions of feeling(s).

Once, as a child, I would weep for compassion and understanding. And Hell was the inferno of my frustration. But the world is clearer to me now, and many of its features, more easily definable.

1965

Also by Amiri Baraka/LeRoi Jones and available from Akashic Books

BLACK MUSIC

256 pages, trade paperback reissue, $16.95
The sequel to Amiri Baraka's seminal work of music criticism, *Blues People*. Featuring a new introduction by the author and an interview by Calvin Reid.

"Jones has learned—and this has been very rare in jazz criticism—to write about music as an artist."   —Nat Hentoff

TALES

160 pages, trade paperback reissue, $15.95
A provocative 1967 short story collection, featuring a new introduction by Henry Louis Gates Jr.

"Jones triumphs because he is consistently able to inspire language wiht new life and rhythm."
                                                —*Saturday Review*

HOME: SOCIAL ESSAYS

288 pages, trade paperback reissue, $15.95
A seminal Jones/Baraka literary land mine, featuring a new introduction by the author.

"Jones/Baraka usually speaks as a Negro—and always as an American. He is eloquent, he is bold. He demands rights—not conditional favors."   —*New York Times Book Review*

TALES OF THE OUT & THE GONE

200 pages, trade paperback original, $16.95
Short Stories. An *Essence* magazine best seller.

"In his prose as in his poetry, Baraka is at his best a lyrical prophet of despair who transfigures his contentious racial and political views into a transcendent, 'outtelligent' clarity."
                        —*New York Times Book Review* (Editors' Choice)

Printed and bound by CPI Group (UK) Ltd, Croydon, CR0 4YY